THE BRYDONS IN A PICKLE

The man found three determined people and a dog too much for him.

Page 124

The Brydons
In A Pickle

by

KATHLEEN FIDLER

Illustrated by

T. R. FREEMAN

LUTTERWORTH PRESS
LONDON

FOR

CATHERINE PINION

*Set and printed in Great Britain by Tonbridge
Printers Ltd., Peach Hall Works, Tonbridge,
Kent, in Old Style twelve on thirteen point*

CONTENTS

Chapter One

A GAME OF CROSS-PURPOSES

IT was a sunny Friday afternoon at the end of the summer term. The pleasant little village of Milchester echoed to the voices of children calling to each other as they hurried home from school on the very last day before the glorious summer holidays began. At One Elm Cottage, half-way up the hill and next door to Beechacres, the big house which was now St. Jonathan's Children's Hospital, Miss Marsden was busy cutting bread and butter for tea, for the Brydons were as healthy and hungry as most young people are. The five of them—Roger and Ruth, the twins Simon and Susan, and Dan—lived with Miss Marsden at One Elm Cottage. At the Convalescent Hospital for children next door, their mother, Dr. Brydon, was the resident doctor. Miss Marsden looked after the Brydon family for her, so she could carry on her own great work among sick children. Professor Brydon, the children's father, was a specialist in queer oriental diseases, and his work frequently carried him far afield to countries in the east. The Brydons were very proud of their father and mother, and were quite happy living with Miss Marsden, dear jolly " Marsdie " to them, for, as Ruth maintained, in One Elm Cottage and St. Jonathan's Hospital they had " the best of both worlds " in their mother and Marsdie too.

Dan Brydon came dashing up the hill, whirling his school-bag on the end of its broken strap. He burst into the kitchen of One Elm Cottage chanting as loudly as his lungs would let him the old rhyme famous among Lancashire school children :

> " Holiday, holiday, hoo !
> The cat's gone to schoo'!
> Broke the teacher's knob stick
> At half-past two.
> Holiday, holiday, hoo ! "

He flung his school-bag upon the old wooden settle, and rummaged in the depths of the bag for a rather crumpled paper, which he handed triumphantly to Miss Marsden.

" Here you are, Marsdie. Here's my school report. I've got ' Excellent ' for Nature Study," he announced very proudly.

Marsdie put down the bread knife and prepared to look at the paper.

" Splendid, Dan ! Let me look. What else ? "

" And a ' Very Good ' for History," Dan pointed out with satisfaction.

Miss Marsden beamed. History was her favourite subject. " Your father and mother will be pleased," she said.

Roger Brydon, Dan's eldest brother, now at London University, leaned over Marsdie's shoulder and surveyed the report too.

" Oh, but what do I see for Arithmetic and English Grammar ? " he queried. " 'Fair only'. ' Improving'. And I think we had better draw a veil over Spelling, don't you, Marsdie ? "

" What does spelling matter anyway, so long as people know what you mean, Roger Brydon ! " Dan protested indignantly.

" Don't tease him, Roger," Marsdie said gently. " My spelling is a bit rocky at times too. What does the general report say ? ' Dan is showing good progress'. Well, that's very gratifying, I'm sure."

Dan nodded with a certain self-righteousness. " Yes, I didn't spend so much time talking to Sam Mitton this term."

" Very sensible of you, Dan," Ruth approved.

" No. I let him talk to me instead," Dan told them, not in the least conscious that there was anything funny about this remark.

When they had all finished laughing, Marsdie asked, " Well, now holidays have begun for everyone, have you made any plans ? "

" It would be nice if we could go away for a holiday, wouldn't it ? " Susan said rather wistfully.

Marsdie looked a little troubled. " Holidays are pretty expensive for a big family nowadays, Susan. You're all beginning to cost a lot more for education, you know," she reminded them.

" Oh, I didn't mean an expensive holiday at a hotel, but *making* a holiday for ourselves," Susan hastened to add.

" Like camping, eh, Susan ? " Simon, her twin, suggested. Simon and Susan always understood each other very well.

" Or the caravan holiday we had," Ruth added. " Something different from the usual kind of holiday."

" I'm afraid we can't borrow a caravan this time, Ruth. Mr. Braddock lent us our last caravan and he's on tour with his circus. Besides, it takes quite a lot of petrol to run a caravan. I don't think we'd have enough," Marsdie reminded them.

" And the Scouts will be camping next week

and will take all their tents with them," Roger pointed out too.

" Perhaps we might go cycling and stay at Youth Hostels," Simon suggested.

Miss Marsden shook her head thoughtfully. " There might be a difficulty about that, Simon. Most people are on holiday just now, and I fear the Youth Hostel accommodation will be booked up for weeks ahead. But we might think about it for another time."

" Mm." Simon nodded his head in agreement. " I quite see that, Marsdie. Well, we'll just have to go on short cycling trips in as many different directions as possible, whenever it's a fine day, and sleep at home."

" That's a good idea, Simon." Ruth seconded the suggestion. " We'll have a lot of picnics."

" We might start to-morrow by going to Whalley Abbey," Simon continued, enlarging his idea, now that he had Ruth's backing. Susan, however, pulled a little face.

" Whalley Abbey ? Oh, Simon, not *again !* "

" Why not ? It's a very pleasant place." Simon upheld his selection stoutly.

" You're quite right, Simon," Ruth agreed with him. " But we shan't be able to go there to-morrow."

" Why not ? "

" Because we're all invited out to tea,"
Ruth told them.

" Oh, where ? " Roger asked, looking up in
surprise.

" Mrs. Hallam wants us all to go to Beechacres."

Mrs. Hallam was Mr. Cameron's stout,
kindly housekeeper. Beechacres was Mr.
Cameron's house before he gave it to the
hospital. He still continued to live there,
retaining several rooms for himself. He and
Mrs. Hallam were among the Brydons' best
friends.

Dan looked rather disgruntled at Ruth's
news. " But we can go and have tea with
Mrs. Hallam at any old time . . . when it's a
rainy day," he declared with his usual blunt
candour. " To-morrow's going to be warm
and sunny."

" But Mrs. Hallam wants us specially
to-morrow, because she's expecting her
brother, the Captain, she calls him," Ruth
explained.

Roger appeared considerably surprised. " I
never knew Mrs. Hallam had a brother," he
declared.

" Let alone one who's a captain," Simon
added.

" What kind of a captain ? " Dan asked
with curiosity. " Army or Navy ? "

" He must have something to do with ships, because Mrs. Hallam said he was taking a short holiday *ashore*, and he'd written to see if he could come to see her at Beechacres," Ruth told them all.

" Well, this *is* news ! " Susan declared.

Everyone was very surprised to learn about Mrs. Hallam's seafaring brother. True, from time to time Mrs. Hallam made mention of her relations, but it was generally by their Christian names,—Tom, or Bill, or Lizzie, and she seemed to assume that the Brydons knew all about them.

" Mrs. Hallam had something of a twinkle in her eye when she told me," Ruth admitted, " but she said she'd like us all to meet the Captain."

" What's his other name ? " Dan asked bluntly.

" Fletcher. The same as Mrs. Hallam's before she was married. Bill Fletcher."

" Captain Bill Fletcher. Mm ! " Roger said thoughtfully. " Of course we must all go to tea. It would never do to hurt Mrs. Hallam's feelings. She's such a good sort."

" You'll probably find Captain Fletcher very interesting. Most seagoing people are. I'm quite looking forward to meeting him," Marsdie declared happily, and the others found themselves agreeing with her too.

The following day saw everyone seated round the tea-table in Mrs. Hallam's bright kitchen. Mrs. Hallam sat at the head of her table, pouring out the tea, and every now and again beaming at her brother, who was at the other end of the table, with Miss Marsden sitting next to him.

Captain Fletcher was very bronzed and had twinkling blue eyes, a little like Mrs. Hallam's. Though he was of stout build, he seemed, nevertheless, very alert and agile, and he had a way of putting his head sideways to look at anyone when he asked a question which reminded Miss Marsden of a very intelligent robin. He wore a trim navy-blue suit, double-breasted, with black buttons, and if Dan felt a trifle disappointed at the absence of gold braid, he did not voice his thoughts aloud.

" Yes, Miss Marsden, it's ten years since I was last in Milchester," Captain Fletcher said in a big booming voice that Roger thought must sound most impressive through a megaphone.

" Is it really, Captain Fletcher ? " Miss Marsden said.

" Aye, ma'am, it's all of that. You see, during the war there was more work for me and my boat down south."

Roger wrinkled his forehead in a puzzled

little frown. " But I thought northern docks were more used during the war because of the heavy bombing in London," he remarked.

Captain Fletcher granted the common-sense of this by a nod of his head, but added, " It all depended on what cargo we were carrying, you see."

" Oh, yes, yes, of course," Roger said hastily, unwilling to be considered ignorant. " What was your cargo, Captain Fletcher ? "

" Sometimes coal, sometimes china clay from Cornwall. Sometimes iron ore or slates or bricks. Whatever I was needed to carry, I carried. But now I mean to come back to Lancashire, to my own country, for the remainder of my days."

" So you're thinking of retiring, Captain Fletcher ? " Ruth asked him.

" Aye," Captain Fletcher nodded. " But before I settle down, I thought I'd take a good holiday and look up old friends and relations like Polly here."

Roger could not restrain a chuckle. He had never heard Mrs. Hallam called Polly before. He was sitting next to her, and whispered, " Goodness, Mrs. Hallam, to think I never knew you were called Polly ! Polly ! Pretty Poll ! "

Mrs. Hallam shook her fist at him. " Eh,

Roger Brydon, if ever you get hold of a thing, you've never done teasing."

Captain Fletcher smiled at his sister. " And very well Polly looks, too," he said with approval. " It must be having all you young folk about her. Well, as my mother used to say . . ."

Before Captain Fletcher had time to finish, the Brydons had risen as one man and chanted in chorus, " And she was a wise woman ! "

Captain Fletcher was utterly astonished. He looked from one to another of the laughing faces.

" Well, I'm blest ! How *did* you know what I was going to say next ? " he demanded.

The Brydons could not help laughing again.

" You see, Captain Fletcher, we've been listening to Mrs. Hallam saying exactly the same thing now for years. ' As my mother used to say, and she was a wise woman . . .' " Ruth quoted again.

" Aye, that's it." Captain Fletcher laughed in his turn. " I suppose certain sayings do cling to families."

" But do go on, please," Miss Marsden begged him.

" Well, she used to say, ' If you want to stay a chicken, you mustn't run round wi' old hens ', " the Captain finished his quotation rather selfconsciously.

A great burst of laughter greeted this gem of common-sense once uttered by Mrs. Hallam's wise mother.

" But I'm glad to see Polly so comfortably fixed, and I shan't let ten years go by again before I come to see you all, you may be sure," Captain Fletcher promised them.

" Does it seem very strange to be ashore again, Captain Fletcher ? " Susan asked.

The Captain regarded her with a slightly puzzled expression, as if he did not know quite what to make of the question.

" No, not very. I often get ashore, you know, many an evening," he replied.

It was the Brydons' turn to look rather puzzled.

" What's the name of your ship, Captain Fletcher ? " Dan asked.

" The *Pride of Lancashire,*" the Captain announced proudly.

" What an unusual name ! What kind of ship is she ? " Simon asked with interest.

" She's a Yorkshire short boat," the Captain stated in a matter-of-fact tone.

" A Yorkshire short boat ? I've never heard of that kind of ship before," Simon replied frankly. " I suppose she's called that because she was built at a Yorkshire port."

" Aye, she probably was," Captain Fletcher agreed. " She's a good steady dependable craft."

" What size is she ? " Roger asked.

" Oh, the usual size for a Yorkshire short boat. Fifty odd feet long and just under fourteen feet beam," the Captain told them casually.

" Beam ? What does that mean ? " Susan asked.

" Oh, her width, I suppose you'd call it," Captain Fletcher explained.

" Surely she's a very narrow boat ? " Simon asked, puzzled.

Captain Fletcher seized on his last two words. " A narrow boat ? Nay, Simon, the ones they call ' narrow boats ' are only seven feet in the beam. They use narrow boats more in the south."

The Brydons and Miss Marsden were looking still more and more mystified, when Dan came along with the question he had been waiting to ask for a long time.

" What speed does the *Pride of Lancashire* go, Captain Fletcher ? How many knots can she make ? " Dan very proudly aired this seamanlike query.

The Captain gave it his due consideration. " Well, when she's moving well, about three miles an hour, maybe," he gave as his verdict.

"It's not allowed, because of the wash, you know."

The others just stared at each other with wide-open eyes.

"Now, Captain Fletcher, you're just pulling our land-lubbers' legs," Roger accused him.

"Nay, lad, I'm not," the Captain replied, just as puzzled by their incredulity. "The *Pride of Lancashire* can do her steady three miles with the best."

Dan was looking most disappointed. Certainly it seemed as if the Captain commanded no Greyhound of the Atlantic.

"But can't you do *more* than three miles

an hour, Captain Fletcher?" he almost begged.

"Aye, if I was in open water I could, lad, but it's not allowed, because of the wash, you know."

"The wash!" Susan exclaimed, her thoughts flying immediately to the laundry, but she asked no further questions for fear of being thought desperately ignorant.

Captain Fletcher went on to explain to them, "Aye, she's a trim little craft, right enough, and I've had her converted from a cargo boat and done up with extra cabin space and fittings, so that I can live aboard her now I've retired."

Again the Brydons opened their eyes wide in astonishment. It seemed rather ridiculous for one elderly gentleman to have a whole big ship to himself for his retirement. They pictured him all alone on board with a huge expanse of empty deck-space about him.

"Really?" was all Miss Marsden could find to say.

"Aye. I didn't see any sense in paying away a mint o' money for a house when I'd a good home already in my boat. Besides, I can cast off now and then and cruise round and see my old cronies," Captain Fletcher explained.

" You've got your head screwed on all right, Bill," Mrs. Hallam said admiringly, in complete agreement with her brother's strange intentions.

Miss Marsden was struggling helplessly with the idea of the Captain weighing anchor, steering the ship, fuelling the boilers, watching the engine gauges, all by himself.

" But what about your crew, Captain Fletcher ? Are they staying with you ? " she asked.

" I shan't need any crew, ma'am. I can manage to work the *Pride of Lancashire* by myself pretty well."

Dan voiced the thoughts of them all. " What ! All that big ship by yourself ? " he cried, his eyes big with wonder.

" Well, I might take an old friend along with me now and again to give me a hand when I come to the locks, if I decide to shift my moorings," the Captain conceded.

" Locks ? Moorings ? I don't understand." It was Ruth's turn now to be bewildered.

" Locks are where you rise from one level of water to another, Ruth," the Captain explained kindly. " In the Cut, you know."

" The Cut ? " Susan and Simon cried together.

" Aye. That's what Lancashire people call the canal, you understand."

Suddenly daylight dawned at once for everyone.

" Oh, well I never ! It's a canal ! "

" What sillies we've been ! "

" The *Pride of Lancashire* is a canal boat ! "

Exclamations of understanding mingled with laughter at the way Captain Fletcher had unintentionally taken them all in.

" We thought you had a big ocean-going steamer, Captain Fletcher," Dan told him.

It was the Captain's turn to laugh heartily.

" Ha, ha ! Nay, lad, the *Pride of Lancashire's* a canal boat right enough. Whatever made you all think anything different ? "

Mrs. Hallam was sitting very quietly smiling to herself. Roger turned and regarded her suspiciously.

" Mrs. Hallam, I see a naughty twinkle in your eye. I suspect you've been having us on a little bit of string all this time," he told her.

Mrs. Hallam disclaimed all intention to deceive them.

" Nay, Roger, it was *you* who made up your minds that Bill commanded a big ship. I never said nowt."

" No, you never said *nowt*," Roger agreed. " You just let us go on blissfully in our mistaken notion. Oh, Polly dear, Polly dear ! "

" Now, Roger, stop teasing," Mrs. Hallam ordered.

Captain Hallam was continuing to tell them more about his boat and his plans.

" Aye, she's a grand canal boat, and I couldn't give her up when it came to retiring. So I've made arrangements to put her on the Leeds and Liverpool Canal and to take her up the Skipton later on, so I shan't be far away from you all. It's bonnie country up yonder, and I'll be near Polly, and still be able to live afloat and see some of my old friends on the canal from time to time."

" Once a sailor, always a sailor, eh, Captain Fletcher ? " Miss Marsden remarked gaily.

" Aye, that's right, ma'am," Captain Fletcher admitted.

" Where is the *Pride of Lancashire* now ? " Simon asked.

" She's lying at Cherry Tree Wharf near Blackburn. I've just had her refitted and repainted."

" Oh, I should like to see your boat, Captain Fletcher," Dan exclaimed. The family averred that Dan was always an expert at angling an invitation for himself.

" So you shall, Dan. And what about taking a trip in her, too ? " Captain Fletcher asked surprisingly.

Both Dan and Susan began to jump up and down with excitement.

"Oh, Captain Fletcher, could we? Could we, Marsdie?" Susan begged.

"If Captain Fletcher really means it," Marsdie smiled at him.

"Of course I do!" the Captain replied heartily. "I'll take you all on as crew, and you can help me to work the *Pride of Lancashire* from Blackburn to Liverpool. I've some business in Liverpool in a short time, and I may as well make the trip that way as by train."

Marsdie hesitated. "Were you inviting just the boys, Captain Fletcher?" she asked. She could not keep a slight note of anxiety from creeping into her voice.

"No, no, Miss Marsden. You and the lasses can come as well. Polly here, too, if she has a mind."

"But where would you put us all? I mean, where would we all sleep?" Miss Marsden asked, in amazement at this rather wholesale invitation.

"There's cabin accommodation aboard the *Pride of Lancashire* for four. I've had a two-berth cabin built in forrad, and there are two berths in the after cabin as well. So you ladies could sleep aboard all right."

"And the boys? Perhaps we could borrow

a tent for them and you ? " Miss Marsden planned.

Captain Fletcher looked rather alarmed. " Borrow a tent ? " he cried. " But then, I'd have to sleep in the tent too. Eh, bless you, Miss Marsden, I've never slept in a tent in my life, and I don't think I'd take kindly to it at my age. I never sleep as comfortable as when there's a stretch of good water beneath me."

" Then what are we to do about it ? We can't deprive you of your bunk," Marsdie declared, slightly bewildered.

Captain Fletcher snapped his fingers to indicate he had hit upon a solution.

" I'll tell you what we'll do. We'll tow a butty boat behind."

" A butty boat ! What's that ? " everybody cried.

" It's a cargo boat that the motor boat takes in tow. I've just sold my old one to Bob Bates, but he's away on a trip just now, so he won't be wanting her for a week or two. There's a cabin in the butty boat too, wi' bunks for four."

Everyone regarded this as the ideal solution, but Dan alone seemed rather miserable about it.

" Only four ! " he cried in a disappointed tone. " Oh, then Sam Mitton won't be able to come."

Everyone else looked rather sorry, too.

" Who is Sam Mitton ? " the Captain wanted to know.

" He's Dan's special chum. He's always been with us on every excursion we've ever had," Ruth explained.

" Aye, he's almost part of the family, Bill. Couldn't you squeeze the little lad in somewhere ? " Mrs. Hallam put in a good word for Sam Mitton herself. " He'd have been here for tea to-day, but he had to go to Preston with his mother to get a new coat."

Captain Fletcher scratched his head. " Well, 'appen I could sling a hammock . . ." he was beginning, when Roger interrupted him.

" I have it ! Your little bivvy tent, Marsdie. It folds up quite small, and if we could moor the boat near a quiet meadow then I could sleep in the bivvy tent, and make room for Sam aboard the butty boat with Dan."

" That's champion, Roger," Mrs. Hallam applauded. " Then there'll be room for all of us."

" All of us ? Do you mean you're really coming too, Mrs. Hallam ? " Ruth cried in delight. Mrs. Hallam was her especial friend.

" I think I'd better come to help Miss Marsden to keep you all in order. Dr. Brydon told me only yesterday that it was high time I took a holiday, and it's a real good chance while Mr. Cameron is away too. I can fix up with Sarah Jane Bentham to come to Beech-acres and do the cooking for a week. She used to be cook at the Rectory, and she'll manage grand."

" It will be fun to have you with us, Mrs. Hallam," Miss Marsden said, very pleased. Mrs. Hallam was always so reliable, so com-forting, so good natured, that she was an asset to any expedition.

" Well, as my mother used to say——" Mrs. Hallam began, and waited for the Brydons to continue.

" And she was a wise woman," the Brydons obediently chorused.

" She used to say, ' You're never really old while you can enjoy a new experience '. We'll be ready to join you bag and baggage when you want us, Bill."

" Then we'd better fix on Wednesday of next week," the Captain said at once. " I'll be waiting for you aboard the *Pride of Lancashire* at the Cherry Tree Wharf, near Blackburn. Bring a couple of bicycles with you."

" Bicycles ! " everyone cried. This seemed such a strange thing to take on a canal trip.

" They're handy for cycling ahead to get the locks ready for the boats coming along, or for running into the towns to do a bit of shopping. We can easily stow them aboard the butty boat."

"It will be fun. Thanks such a lot, Captain Fletcher. Hurry up, Wednesday!" came from all the Brydons.

As for Dan, he was already dancing a vigorous sailor's hornpipe at the thought that Sam Mitton was to join them too.

Chapter Two

THE BRYDONS GET THEIR CANAL LEGS

THE following Wednesday Miss Marsden drove the Brydons and all their gear in the shooting-brake to Cherry Tree Wharf on the outskirts of Blackburn. As they drew alongside the wharf, which was black with coal dust from the unloading of coal barges, they saw a gaily-painted boat lying in the water just below them. A sombre, more workmanlike barge was secured to her astern. They would have had no difficulty in recognizing the *Pride of Lancashire* and her attendant butty boat, even if there had been no name picked out in yellow and red lettering round her stern.

" Eh, there are Bill's two boats," Mrs. Hallam announced quite unnecessarily as she stepped from the shooting-brake. " There he is, waving to us."

Captain Fletcher had appeared on deck and came forward to welcome them.

" Good-day, Miss Marsden. Hallo, Polly !
Well, there you all are, and it's nice to see my
crew so ready and punctual."

He hastened to put a gang-plank between
the wharf and the boat so that the ladies could
step aboard more easily. He held out his
hand to assist Miss Marsden.

" Welcome aboard the *Pride of Lancashire*,"
he said, with a beaming smile.

" Thank you, Captain Fletcher," Miss Marsden said as she stepped aboard. " We think
your boat is very suitably named. No wonder
you're proud of her."

" It's the very nicest canal boat I've ever
seen," Susan declared.

Captain Fletcher was very pleased at these
compliments paid to his boat. " Thank you,
ma'am. Thank you, Susan. She's not a bad
little craft. Come aboard, Polly." He gave
his hand to his sister, who was carrying a
large basket of provisions. " Well, how are
you ? "

" Glad to see you and your boat, Bill."

Ruth had followed Mrs. Hallam aboard, and
she and Susan were already busy looking at
the outside of the *Pride of Lancashire's*
painted cabin.

" Oh, what beautiful painted panels ! "
Ruth cried. " Look, Marsdie ! Look, Susan!
What a beautiful spray of roses ! And there's

"Why, you could eat off the floor!"

even a landscape with a castle and a river.
Why, the boat's just like a floating caravan."

Captain Fletcher was very gratified at
Ruth's admiration.

" Aye, the time was when every cabin on a
canal boat had its painted panels with castles
and sprays of flowers, but nowadays folk go
in for grey paint and utility, and there's nowt
to distinguish one canal boat from another."
He could not help giving a little regretful sigh.
" I like my bright paintwork, I do," Captain
Fletcher declared. " But come and have a
look at your living quarters, Miss Marsden,
and see if they suit you." He led the way
down the short ladder into the cabin. " Here
you are. Here's your dining-saloon and
sitting-room, with the galley attached."

The cosy little cabin glowed with brightness
and fresh paint and highly polished wood-
work. Even Mrs. Hallam caught her breath
at its spotless cleanliness.

" Oh, I never imagined a saloon on a barge
could be so comfortable," Marsdie exclaimed
in delight. " There's even a divan with
cushions too."

" Why, you could eat off the floor," Mrs.
Hallam declared with approbation, still staring
around her.

" Aye, Polly, but you don't have to,"
Captain Fletcher laughed, letting down a

fixture of polished wood. " See, this table hinged against the wall will let down for meals. It has folding legs at the corners. There's even a leaf you can put in to extend it."

The Brydons stared at its compactness.

" How very handy," Marsdie declared.

" It will be splendid, provided you don't fold it up again with the dishes still on it, Marsdie," Roger teased her. The Brydon family always made gentle fun of Marsdie's absentmindedness.

" I just love these red-checked curtains with cushions to match," Ruth declared.

Susan had picked up a large painted can with a handle. It, too, was decorated with a spray of red poppies.

" It's just like a giant hot-water jug with a spout and lid," she cried. " What do you use these cans for, Captain Fletcher ? There's an open one, too."

" They're water cans, Susan. The open can is a dipper for lifting water out of the canal to scrub the deck. The other covered one is kept entirely for drinking water and cooking. You have to fill that up from the fifteen-gallon drinking-water tank in the forepeak. Every two or three days we get that filled up by a hose pipe from a proper tap-water supply ashore."

" Oh, so we don't have to drink the canal water, then ? " Dan asked with interest.

"Goodness me, no, boy!" Captain Fletcher said, pulling a face. "Don't you go trying it on either, or you will get pains in your tummy!"

Mrs. Hallam was investigating the comforts of the saloon.

"Eh, Bill, you've got a proper coal stove," she exclaimed.

"Of course I have, Polly. How did you think I kept warm in winter? There's no cosier place in the world than this cabin when the lamp's lit, and the curtains drawn, and the wind's whistling away over the top of the boat."

"It's like a proper little sitting-room, and there I thought you were roughing it," she declared.

"Here's the kitchen, in here," Ruth cried with delight, peering into the alcove next to the saloon.

"You mean the galley, my lass," Captain Fletcher reproved her. "Yes, there's an oil-burning cooking-stove that you may find useful, Polly."

"Why, there's a kitchen sink, too," Ruth exclaimed.

Dan Brydon regarded this amenity of civilization with distinct disgust. "Oh, bother!" he cried, "then there'll still be washing-up to do."

Sam Mitton, who was peeping over his shoulder, regarded the situation with greater philosophy.

" Cheer up, Dan. It'll be no worse than at home."

" No, but you've less chance of getting away from it on a barge," Dan said candidly.

Captain Fletcher proudly lifted the plug in the aluminium sink and said, " There ! You can drain the water away into the canal when you've finished. Not many canal boats have a contraption like that. I had that put in specially."

" Just look at all the shelves with pots and pans and jars ! It's all so neat and clean," Susan exclaimed with pleasure.

" Just step across to the other side of the gangway," Captain Fletcher directed, opening a door.

" What is it ? A big cupboard ? " Simon asked.

Captain Fletcher shook his head. " No. This is your bathroom."

" With a real wash-basin ! " Ruth cried.

" And towel rails too, and a sponge rack," Marsdie exclaimed with delight. " And everything painted white and so clean and shining."

" So *we* have to get washed as well as the dishes," Dan remarked gloomily. " We might just as well stay at home."

35

" Dan, you're a dirty, scruffy little boy,"
Susan told him. " I never knew anyone hate
water so much except for fishing in."

" There's many a bonnie stretch of the
canal where the water's clean and clear like a
river, after you leave the towns behind,"
Captain Fletcher informed them. " You'll be
able to swim there, if you have a mind to do,
so I hope you boys have brought your
swimming trunks."

" Rather ! " Roger and Simon said.

" We'd no idea you had such a charming
home, Captain Fletcher. No wonder you
don't want to leave it. It's awfully good of
you to have us all aboard," Miss Marsden said.

" I reckon any friends of Polly's are friends
of mine, too, and you're all right welcome,"
Captain Fletcher replied gallantly. " And
now, maybe it 'ud be as well if you got your
luggage out of the car and stowed aboard.
Come along. I'll give you a hand."

Their reappearance on deck was greeted by
a joyous barking from the wharf side.

" Hallo, have you brought a dog ? " Captain
Fletcher asked them.

" Not to my knowledge," Marsdie declared,
greatly surprised.

" But that's Jonathan's bark. Why, yes, it
is Jonathan ! " Roger exclaimed. " How on
earth did he get here ? "

Jonathan rushed up and down the edge of the wharf, at great peril of tumbling into the canal, then took a flying leap and landed on deck, where he ran from one to another, jumping up at them and licking their hands, as though they had all been reunited after a long separation.

Susan fixed Dan with her eye. "Dan Brydon, you've got an awful guilty look."

"I couldn't help bringing him, really I couldn't," Dan confessed. "He came up just when we were going to drive off, while you were all busy saying good-bye to Mother and Sister Jones, and he looked so sad and miserable that I just *had* to hide him under the seat at the back, and he stayed there quietly all the way. I think he knew he was hiding."

"Really, Dan, you are the limit! What are we going to do with Jonathan now?" Ruth asked.

"You can let him come too," Captain Fletcher said good-naturedly. "I reckon he's the only passenger who won't be asking for a sleeping berth. Besides, most canal boats carry a dog. I had one for nearly ten years, and I hadn't the heart to get another after he died. Come on, Jonathan lad, you're welcome too."

As though Jonathan knew that Captain Fletcher had interceded on his behalf, he dashed up to him and licked his hand so vigorously that the Captain said, " Hold on, lad, or you'll lick my freckles off."

The Brydons returned to the shooting-brake, and brought their luggage and the two bicycles down to the boat.

" We've just brought what you advised us to, Captain Fletcher, no more," Miss Marsden said.

" That's right, ma'am. You'll mostly be able to buy what you want as you go through the villages and towns, but it's handy to have a little stock of flour and sugar, and so on, beside you. You can put the provisions in the larder below the after-deck. It's nice and cool there and you'll find a meat-safe. Now, if you've got everything aboard, I've made arrangements with the garage folk at the end of the street to keep your shooting-brake for you, Miss Marsden. They're decent, honest folk and they'll look after it all right."

Miss Marsden went to garage the car, and when she returned she found the others had stowed everything away " proper ship-shape," as the Captain declared.

" Now we're all ready to start," he announced. " Would you like to try your hand at working the engine, Roger ? "

" Gosh ! Wouldn't I ? You try me," Roger said.

" Then Simon can take the tiller of the butty boat and the two little lads can help him," the Captain arranged.

Simon was quite thrilled to have this position of responsibility. The boys scrambled aboard the butty boat.

" Right ! All set ! " Simon cried.

" I'll take the tiller of this boat. The tow lines between the two boats are fixed already, so you only need to steer the butty boat just as I steer the leading boat," the Captain instructed Simon.

" I'll do just what you do," Simon called back.

" All right. We'll get under way now."

Captain Fletcher showed Roger how to start up the engine.

" Cast off the mooring-ropes now, Sam and Dan. That's the way. Don't leave them lying across the deck. Coil them up like this. That's the way. Now we're ready."

The engine began to throb, and the two barges began to slide away from Cherry Tree Wharf.

" We're really off ! Hurrah ! " the Brydons cried. Simon, on the butty boat, struck up a sea-shanty : " Blow the man down, bullies, blow the man down," and soon everyone else joined in, " Yo ho, blow the man down."

To this rousing chorus they headed downstream. The beat of the engine increased its pace a little, and soon the *Pride of Lancashire* was moving south-west at a steady three miles an hour.

When they had cruised awhile, Susan, seated up in the forepeak, gave Captain Fletcher a hail.

" Here's another barge coming in the opposite direction, Captain Fletcher."

Captain Fletcher took a quick look at the oncoming craft.

" It's not rightly a barge, Susan. It's a Yorkshire short boat, the same as mine. Aye, that'll be Tom Ellis's boat, the *Polly Peachum*. He'll be tying up at Stanworth for a load of stone from the quarries, I reckon."

" Do you know everybody on the canal, Captain Fletcher ? " Susan asked.

" Aye, pretty well nigh on all on 'em, just like you know all the folk in Milchester, Susan. We give each other the news when we're passing. Listen ! Tom's stopping his engine. This is where we stop ours too and drift till we're alongside."

Captain Fletcher signalled to Roger and to Miss Marsden, who was assisting Roger with the engine, and the throb died down, and slowly the two boats began to draw level in the water. As soon as they were within comfortable hailing distance, the owner of the oncoming barge began his conversation with Captain Fletcher, a conversation that could be heard by anyone within a hundred yards. Susan thought she knew now why the Captain's voice had such a booming sound.

" Hi, Cap'n Bill, the *Pride of Lancashire's* looking very smart.   Got your re-fit finished?"

" Aye, Tom.   How's the missus and the bairns ? "

" Below decks.   Here they come tumbling up to meet you."

A pleasant-faced woman, with a laughing baby in her arms, and a boy of about four came on deck from the saloon.

" Hallo, Cap'n Bill !   Where are you bound ? " the little lad cried in the approved fashion of canal-boat folk.

" Liverpool, young Tom," the Captain said with a grin, throwing the child a treacle caramel which the boy caught very cleverly.

" Hallo, Annie !   My, the babby's grown ! " the Captain cried.

Tom Ellis grinned.   " Aye, Bill, and you've suddenly got a grown-up family too."

Fletcher laughed.   " Aye, not bad, eh ? " He stretched out a boat-hook and grappled the *Polly Peachum* so that the boats should not drift apart until the conversation was ended.   " I'm carrying passengers this trip, Tom."

" Well, now, I never thought you'd go in for being a pleasure boat, Bill," Tom Ellis chuckled.

" Oh, these are just a few of my friends I'm taking for a little cruise afore I tie up for good." The Captain indicated Miss Marsden and the Brydons with a flourish of his hand.

" Aye, I heard tell you were retiring," Tom told him.

" That's right. But I'm still going to live on the Cut in the *Pride of Lancashire*, Tom. I couldn't abide a town at my time of life. Who's below you downstream ? Do you know ? " Captain Fletcher asked.

" Aye. Willie Atherton. He's waiting for you coming down. He's at the top lock at Johnson's Hillock."

" We'll be moving down then," the Captain said, loosing his hold with the boat-hook upon the *Polly Peachum*. " Willie won't have long to wait for us. Here, young Tom. Catch this bit o' toffee." Again he threw a caramel to the little boy, who grinned with pleasure. " So long, Tom. Cheerio, Mrs. Ellis."

" Good-bye, Cap'n Bill," Mrs. Ellis and the little lad called, and even the baby waved his hand.

The two boats drifted apart, and both started up their engines again and began to move on, to much friendly waving from the occupants of both. Susan looked up at Captain Fletcher rather shyly.

"Mr. Ellis called you Cap'n Bill. Do you mind terribly if we call you that too?" she asked.

"Most folk call me Cap'n Bill, Susan. I've been thinking it would sound more friendly-like if you all did, too."

"Then we will," the Brydons told him.

Ruth asked, "Did Mr. Ellis say that some-one was waiting for you at a canal lock?"

"Aye. Willie Atherton's at Johnson's Hillock."

"But how does he know *you* are coming down the canal, Cap'n Bill?" Marsdie inquired. Both she and Ruth had been puzzled by this piece of information.

"He doesn't," Cap'n Bill said surprisingly. "You see, Miss Marsden, he wants to come *up* the canal and I want to go *down*. If he waits at the lock for a boat coming down, then the same lock full of water will do for the two of us, to let him up and me down. It's one of the rules of the canal, so we don't waste water that way."

Miss Marsden still looked puzzled. "I'm afraid I don't quite understand," she confessed. Ruth and Susan shook their heads too.

"In a few minutes we shall reach the top

lock, and you'll see what happens then, and it'll make it all clear to you," the Captain reassured them.

In about a quarter of an hour the *Pride of Lancashire* reached Johnson's Hillock. Behind the closed lock gates, in the lock, but at a level of about fifteen feet below them, another boat was waiting.

"We'll tie up here, Simon," Cap'n Bill shouted to Simon at the tiller of the butty boat. "I'll fasten up to that mooring ring. Just let the butty boat come to rest behind us against that bank. Now, Sam and Dan, you nip out and tie us both up. We'll have to wait for Willie Atherton's boat to come up the lock."

Dan and Sam obeyed with alacrity, and Cap'n Bill made sure they knew how to tie the loops of the heavy rope correctly.

"May we go ashore, Cap'n Bill?" Ruth asked.

"Aye. Off wi' the lot of you and watch the *Miranda* coming through. 'Appen we can give a bit of help."

They all tumbled off the boat, including Miss Marsden and Mrs. Hallam, and rushed to look down upon the *Miranda* in the lock below.

"Isn't this fun?" Susan cried.

"It's quite a new thing for us," Marsdie agreed.

" Oh, doesn't the *Miranda* look a long way below us ? " Ruth exclaimed.

" Aye, but she'll soon be level with us. Hallo, Willie ! You can start winding. We're alongside," Cap'n Bill hailed the owner of the *Miranda*, who was not aboard his boat but standing by the lock gates.

" *Winding ?* What does he have to wind, Cap'n Bill ? " Susan asked.

" You see that tool in his hand ? It's a windlass. Some folk call it a crank. It's shaped like the letter L, a bit like a motor car starter. It's a kind of key to open the locks."

Dan went into fits of laughter. " Ha, ha, Cap'n Bill ! A *key* to open the *locks !* "

Captain Fletcher chuckled too. " Aye, you may laugh, Dan, but I'm right. The windlass has got a square socket which fits on to the spindle in that post that works the lock paddles."

" Paddles ! " Miss Marsden exclaimed, looking more mystified than ever. " What are they ? "

" They're sluice doors in the lock gates themselves, Miss Marsden. When you turn yon spindle with the windlass, it raises the doors and lets the water into the lock from the higher level. But before Willie Atherton opens the sluice doors, he sees that the bottom lock gates are shut fast. Watch now."

45

From the lowermost open lock gates a long beam of wood stuck out like a huge handle. Willie Atherton began to push this beam out towards the tow path, and, as he pushed it slowly, the giant doors of the lock began to move inwards towards one another.

" Those are the balance beams that shut the lock gates again," Captain Fletcher explained. " Run and give him a hand, lads. It's not easy work, and canal folk always help each other at the locks."

" We'll help to push too, Mr. Atherton," Roger called to him.

" Thanks, lads," Willie Atherton said, as he stopped for a moment and wiped the perspiration from his brow with a large red-and-white spotted handkerchief.

" Gosh ! It's heavier than you'd think, isn't it ? " Roger cried, applying his weight to the beam.

" Aye, lad. You're pushing against the weight o' the water, you see," Willie Atherton explained.

At last the heavy lock gates met in the middle, and the dovetailed edges closed tightly so that the water could not escape between them. The *Miranda* now lay in the lock itself, with the closed lock gates behind her and the other lock gates before her, also closed, but at a higher level.

" Now the bottom lock gates are shut, we let the water into the lock through the top lock sluices," Cap'n Bill explained to Miss Marsden. " You watch what happens." He called to Willie Atherton. " Hi, Will, let the lads take a turn at winding now. They're my apprentice crew and they've got to learn, I reckon."

Willie gladly ceded the windlass handle to Simon, who started away vigorously enough, but found it took more strength and knack than he had imagined.

" Gosh ! This is stiffer than you'd think, too," he said.

Miss Marsden was watching the upper lock gates. " Oh, the little doors in the gates themselves are all lifting and the water's rushing into the lock from the canal above," she cried.

" It won't sink the *Miranda*, will it ? " Susan asked Captain Fletcher anxiously.

" Not it, my lass ! " the Captain replied with a laugh. " The *Miranda* 'll rise like a cork in the water."

The water roared and surged through the sluices into the lock, and the boat continued to rise. Bit by bit the level of the water came up in the lock, and the *Miranda* with it. At last the water was level with that in the upper reaches of the canal, and it ceased to eddy and swirl about the waiting boat.

" Why, the *Miranda's* level with us now,"
Susan exclaimed. " What happens next,
Cap'n Bill ? "

" Willie Atherton will push on the balance
beams on the gates near to us and swing them
back. Here he comes, with the boys to help
him."

They all pushed the balance beam valiantly
towards the lock.

" Oh, look ! The gates are opening ! "
Marsdie cried.

Willie Atherton jumped aboard the *Miranda*
and started the engine, and the craft nosed
slowly up to the opening gates and began to
lend her weight to open them.

" See, the *Miranda's* pushing her way out
too, and helping to swing the gates back,"
Cap'n Bill pointed out to them.

At last the gates were wide open, and the
Miranda came slowly out towards them and
emerged completely into the upper canal. As
she passed the *Pride of Lancashire*, Willie
Atherton called, " Thanks, folks. Your turn
now."

Captain Fletcher helped Roger to start up
the engine again.

" Get aboard the butty boat now, Simon,
and guide her into the lock after me. Slacken
the tow rope so that both boats can lie
alongside each other in the lock."

Simon did as he was instructed, while Dan and Sam cast off the mooring ropes, and with the Captain's guidance slackened the tow rope too. Miss Marsden, Mrs. Hallam, Ruth and Susan went aboard the *Pride of Lancashire* so as to have the thrill of going through the lock aboard her. Gently Cap'n Bill guided his boat into the lock, and slowly the butty boat drifted in alongside him.

"Well done, Simon!" Cap'n Bill commended him.

"Oh, we're in the lock! We're in the lock!" Susan cried, jigging up and down with excitement.

Captain Fletcher turned to Miss Marsden. "Now, you see, Miss Marsden, when Willie Atherton's boat came up, it left a lock full of water ready for us. We use the same water to go down. That saves a powerful waste of water."

"I'm beginning to understand that now," Marsdie said. "What happens next?"

"We work the locks the other way round. First we shut the top gates behind us."

Again the boys pulled on the beams, with Willie Atherton to assist them this time, and at last the big wooden gates were shut behind the *Pride of Lancashire*.

"Now we've got to drop the level of the water in the lock," Cap'n Bill explained.

" We do that by opening the sluices in the bottom gates now, and letting the water run out of the lock gradually to the lower level of the canal."

" I'll work the windlass," Roger volunteered.

Roger and Simon turned the windlass handle in turn, and the sluices opened little by little, and the water began to pour out from the lock to the canal below.

" Oh ! " cried Susan, as she saw the walls of the lock seemingly rising above her head. " The level of the water's going down in the lock and we're sinking down with it too ! "

" Eh, it's just like going down in a lift," Mrs. Hallam exclaimed, " only it's a bit slower. But it gives you the same queer feeling in your stomach."

" Now, don't go and be canal-sick, Mrs. Hallam," Roger cautioned her with a grin.

The level of the water had sunk to that of the lower canal now, so once again the boys pushed on the balance beams and opened the lower lock gates. On a little forward surge of water, the *Pride of Lancashire* drew clear of the lock and emerged on to the open canal again.

" It's straight sailing for a bit now," Captain Fletcher told them. " I'll let you manage the next pair of locks yourselves, so, if need be, you'd know how to work the boat along."

" Oh, do you mean it, Cap'n Bill ? " Simon asked, delighted.

" Aye. You didn't shape so badly for the first time. With a bit more practice, you'll do quite well. You'll have a chance very soon when we reach Johnson's Bottom lock half a mile further down. Then, after that, we'll think about tying up for a bit while we all have a meal. There's a good smell coming from the galley, Ruth."

Ruth saluted in sailor-like fashion. " Aye, aye, Cap'n Bill. It's stewed steak with mixed vegetables. Mrs. Hallam says it'll be ready once you're through the bottom lock."

" Very well. Once we're through we'll drift on a bit in the direction of Botany Bay. Give me a hail when you're ready to tie up. I'll have the mooring pins handy."

" Botany Bay, Cap'n Bill ? But I thought that was where the convicts used to be sent in olden times. In Australia, you know ? " Sam Mitton said.

" Then you can think again, Sam lad, about this Botany Bay. It's quite near Chorley. After dinner we can tie up there for an hour or two, if Miss Marsden and Polly would like to go ashore and do a bit of shopping in Chorley. You might get a bit of something nice for supper, Polly."

Mrs. Hallam looked quite pleased at the

prospect of shopping in a town. After all, Milchester was not very big, and only had two or three shops.

" I know a shop in Chorley that used to sell grand tripe and cowheels," she said. " Come on, Miss Marsden, let's get dinner over, and then we'll see what Chorley has to offer."

" You've a bit of a walk either way, but it'll stretch your legs after sitting in the boat. Fetch me a couple of ounces of thick twist, will you, Polly? I might manage without my supper, but I couldn't do without my pipe of an evening."

At the second locks the Brydons acquitted themselves very creditably indeed, and the Captain expressed himself as highly satisfied with his crew. After that it was plain sailing for Botany Bay, but they moored first to have dinner. Mrs. Hallam had prepared them an excellent meal, and they all found themselves very ready for it.

" Working the locks makes you jolly hungry," Dan declared.

" It seems like it," Roger remarked, as he passed up his plate for a third helping of pudding. " Don't eat too much, young Dan. We might require you to haul the boat if the engine breaks down."

Dan looked quite alarmed until he saw Roger give Cap'n Bill a mighty wink.

" All the same, I must say you've kept your hand in at the cooking jolly well, Polly," the Captain complimented his sister.

" Every man to his trade," Polly replied, but there was a gleam of satisfaction in her eye.

At Botany Bay they tied up again, and Miss Marsden, Mrs. Hallam and the Brydons went ashore to explore Chorley and to do some shopping, while the Captain remained aboard, meditatively smoking his pipe and exchanging greetings with all and sundry who passed along the canal.

The Brydons were back in plenty of time for tea, bringing all kinds of mysterious and knobby parcels back with them, not forgetting the Captain's thick twist ; then once more the boat got under way.

For another four miles the *Pride of Lancashire* throbbed slowly on, easing gently under Cowling Bridge. Not far from there they reached a nice quiet stretch of the canal, bordered with meadows and an occasional fringe of woodland. In the near distance was a high bracken-crowned hill. Captain Fletcher stopped his engine, and allowed the boat to drift in towards the bank.

" I reckon we've reached the place where we can tie up for the night," he said. " Is this quiet enough for you, Miss Marsden ? "

Miss Marsden looked about her with appreciation. " I think it's just beautiful, with those woodlands on the other side of the towpath ; and there's that pretty village stretching up the hill, near, but not too near."

" Aye, that's Adlington village, and that big hill you can see beyond, towering over the village, is Rivington Pike," Cap'n Bill informed her. " A right beauty spot it is, and a favourite place for picnic parties. Folk come from all over Lancashire to climb the Pike. They tell me that from the top you can see Liverpool on a clear day."

Susan, for whom mountains and hills had always had a strange appeal, looked wistfully at the Pike. " It does look so lovely with all that tawny bracken on it."

" Would you like to climb it, Susan ? " the Captain asked her.

Susan nodded, without saying a word.

" Then suppose we stay tied up here for a day and you can all have a picnic up there to-morrow," the Captain proposed.

This suggestion brought vigorous applause from everyone.

" You must be sure to visit the old Elizabethan barn just beyond Rivington village. It's a wonderful place," Captain Fletcher advised them.

" That does sound jolly. But aren't you coming with us, Cap'n Bill ? " Ruth asked.

Captain Fletcher shook his head. " No, Ruth, my lass, I don't think I will. I've meandered among flat meadows by the canal all my days, and I don't take kindly to hill-climbing now. I'll just have a quiet day aboard the *Pride of Lancashire*, and smoke my pipe and keep a look-out for old friends on the Cut, and pass the time o' day with them. I reckon that's more in my line. But you go and enjoy yourselves."

Mrs. Hallam called from below. " The supper's set ready now. Will you all come below to the saloon or it'll go cold."

" ' Below to the saloon ', mark you ! " Roger exclaimed. " Mrs. Hallam's getting quite nautical."

" Well, I allus said, ' When in Rome, you should learn the language '," Mrs. Hallam told them.

" That is a new variation of an old proverb, Mrs. Hallam," Marsdie laughed.

" Yes, even your wise mother couldn't have thought of a better one than that," Roger teased her.

" Even old proverbs can do wi' a new look at times," Mrs. Hallam declared. " Come on now, folks, squeeze in. There's not much room, but if you tuck your elbows in, four of you can get on that seat alongside the table."

"What a lovely smell!" Dan said appreciatively. "It's onions."

"It's like a supper mi mother allus makes on Saturday night," Sam Mitton told them. "Only it smells better still on a boat, somehow."

"Ruth's cooked this, wi' me to keep an eye on it," Mrs. Hallam informed them.

Susan looked round with quiet delight. "I think the lamplight looks lovely in the cabin. It's all so cosy and home-like. But where's Simon?"

"Here, Susan. Just coming downstairs," Simon said as he came down the ladder in a couple of jumps.

"*Below*, you mean, not *downstairs*," Mrs. Hallam corrected him.

"Sorry, Mrs. Hallam. *Below*. I've been pitching the tent on that little stretch of meadow between us and the place where the trees come down to the water. Roger and I are sleeping there."

"Yes. We thought two of us would be more company," Roger said.

"Hurrah! That gives us the butty boat to ourselves, Sam," Dan exclaimed.

"But what about Cap'n Bill?" Marsdie asked him.

" Oh, it doesn't matter for him. He's one of us. He won't try to boss us like Roger does," Dan said bluntly.

Cap'n Bill acknowledged the delicate nature of the compliment with a bow.

" It did look beautiful from the meadow when you lit the lamps," Simon told them. " The portholes glowed like lovely big lanterns and were reflected in the water, and with the trees standing dark behind us and the sun westering and throwing a rosy light on those stone cottages straggling up the hillside, it made me wish I could paint. I had no idea a canal could be so beautiful."

Captain Fletcher threw Simon a glance of warm approval. " I reckon a canal's like life, Simon lad. It has its lovely quiet bits, and its busy ugly patches too. The day after to-morrow you'll go through Wigan, but think on when you see the water black wi' coal dust and the great dark mills crowding round, that they're just as necessary for life as the quiet waters and green fields. And if you look for it, you'll find a kind of grim beauty there too."

Mrs. Hallam opened her eyes wide. " Eh, Bill, I never knew you were a philosopher."

The Captain smiled a little awkwardly. " Well, Polly, living on a canal boat teaches you a lot. You learn that sooner or later you always pass through the noisy towns back to the good green fields again. But, to come back to earth a bit, that was a grand dish of cow-heel and tripe, Ruth, and I dunno as I ever tasted a better."

Ruth modestly disclaimed the credit. " You can thank Mrs. Hallam and Marsdie really. They brought it from Chorley."

" Eh, but it was Miss Marsden who remembered the onions. I'd have forgotten them," Mrs. Hallam admitted.

" Marsdie ! This feat of memory is incredible ! " Roger declared.

Poor Marsdie was always being teased for her sudden lapses of memory and mind-wandering, when she did the most unaccountable things.

" Oh, I have my moments," Marsdie assured them gaily. " And now, what about a song or two while we wash up the dishes."

Dan was suddenly moved to make a surprising offer. " There isn't room for all of us to be moving around, so if Susan will wash the dishes, Sam and I will dry them. And all the rest of you can sit and sing."

The astonished company regarded Dan with wide-open mouths.

" Dan ! Whatever's come over you ? Do you mean you really *want* to wash up ? " Ruth cried.

" Oh, I have my moments too," Dan

declared with a flourish of the drying-cloth. " Come on, Sam, you get hold of another of these."

" Well, well ! " Roger commented. " The age of miracles is never past. It must be something in the canal air."

" Come along then. Let's start the singing, so that Dan and Sam can have music while they work," Marsdie proposed. " What shall we sing ? "

" ' One More River ', seeing we're in a kind of ark," Ruth suggested.

So, to the tune of " The Animals Went in Two by Two ", Dan and Sam got through their chores, everyone singing cheerfully, including Cap'n Bill.

Chapter Three

THE MYSTERIOUS *CROCUS*

ROGER and Simon slept in the small bivouac tent where the meadow fringed the canal. The night was quiet and undisturbed, and everyone retired early, as there really did seem to be something in the canal air which made for sleep. Marsdie thought it might possibly be the heavy supper of tripe and onions to which they were not accustomed, but the Brydons hotly repudiated this suggestion.

" Never mind, if we go to bed early, we can get up early too, and have a longer day on the top of Rivington Pike," Susan murmured with sleepy satisfaction.

Roger awoke early to the twitter of birds in the nearby wood. The early-morning sunshine still had that hazy quality of pale golden light. From the chimneys of the little village on the hillside smoke was beginning to curl lazily here and there. Roger stood up and stretched himself, and Simon stirred and turned in his sleeping-bag.

" Are you awake, Simon ? " Roger asked in a low voice.

" Yes. Is it terribly early ? " Simon asked, sitting up.

" About six o'clock, I think," Roger said, consulting his wrist-watch.

Simon peered through the open tent flap towards the *Pride of Lancashire*.

" There's no sign of anyone stirring on the boats yet," he commented. " I say ! What a lovely day ! There's something blue and sunny about it, as though it were waiting for something nice to happen."

" It's a perfect morning for a swim," Roger said. " What about it ? "

" Jolly good idea ! But you don't think our splashing about would wake the others, do you ? "

Simon was always thoughtful for the comfort of others.

" We can go downstream a bit, just beyond that bend in the canal where the trees come down to the water," Roger suggested.

" All right. It's lucky we've got our bathing-trunks in the tent with us." Simon leaped up and divested himself of his sleeping-bag. " I'll race you getting ready and running across the meadow to that first tree."

" All right," Roger said, hunting feverishly in his kit bag for his swimming-trunks.

Simon was quicker off his mark, and streaked across the meadow just in front of Roger. He reached the first tree and there was a splash, followed by a second splash, as both dived in, and two heads bobbed up again almost simultaneously above the surface of the water.

" Just beat me to it, didn't you ? " Roger admitted.

" You should have left your bathing-trunks handy the night before, as I did," Simon grinned.

" I vote we have another race, swimming this time," Roger said. " At any rate, on this occasion we shall start equal. We'll race round the bend to the end of that plantation of trees, and we'll make the last tree on the water the finishing post. It should be about three hundred yards away."

" Right ! Get ready, then. One. Two. Three. Go ! " Simon cried.

Side by side they raced, neither able to draw much ahead of the other. If Roger had the longer reach and pull, Simon had made sure that he was nearer the inside of the bend to the canal. Then, just as they came up to the last tree, Roger forged a foot or two ahead.

" Beaten you this time, Simon," he panted.

" Oh, you won all right, Roger," Simon

conceded. " You can move through the water a bit faster than I can yet."

" I'm getting more practice in London than I did in Milchester," Roger confessed. " I joined the University Swimming Club." He pulled himself out of the canal and sat at the edge. Suddenly he exclaimed, " Why, there's another canal boat moored down there."

Simon looked downstream in the direction of his pointing finger.

" She's not quite so spick-and-span-looking as the *Pride of Lancashire*, though."

" No. She looks as if she could do with a coat of paint," Roger agreed. " She's got all her cargo sheeted down with tarpaulins."

" I wonder what she's carrying ? " Simon said, with the interested curiosity of one barge inhabitant about another. " It can't be coal, or they wouldn't have it all covered over with tarpaulins like that."

" There doesn't seem to be anyone about. Let's swim alongside her and take a look," Roger suggested.

The boys swam lazily downstream till they reached the moored barge, the bows of which pointed downstream too. As Roger approached the stern he could make out the dingy lettering of her name, the *Crocus*.

" Mm ! That name isn't very suitable. There's nothing very fresh and spring-like about this craft," he said to Simon in a low voice. "She'd do with a general clean-up, besides a coat of paint. Everything seems very quiet. I don't think there's anyone aboard."

"Yes, there is," Simon told him in a quiet voice. "I saw a face at the starboard port-hole just now. Turn and swim past again and take a look."

The boys turned and began to swim up-stream again. Instinctively they made as little splashing noise as possible, partly from a desire not to attract the attention of the occupants of the boat, and partly due to a reason they could not have explained. Roger's eyes searched the boat as they passed.

"You're right, Simon," he said, as they drew out of hearing of anyone on the boat. "I saw a man's face peer at us, and then disappear as if it had been plucked back in a hurry."

"That's strange, when all the canal people seem so friendly," Simon remarked thought-fully. "They usually give everyone such a cheery greeting when they meet."

"Yes, you'd have thought he'd have put out his head and wished us a bright good-morning, wouldn't you?" Roger agreed.

"Maybe we wakened him up and he's not overjoyed to see us," Simon hazarded a guess.

" Maybe. Perhaps there are unwritten laws in the canal world about waking your neighbours by untimely swimming. We'd better get back to our own boats."

Simon still seemed puzzled. " The *Crocus* is headed downstream," he pointed out. " I wonder why we didn't hear them passing us last night ? You can usually hear Diesel engines quite a distance away."

" We were making a great row singing away in the cabin, remember," Roger reminded him.

Simon nodded. " Yes, of course. In any case they might have been tied up here before we came along."

" Quite possibly, though you'd have thought we would have seen some of the crew about. Anyway, it's no concern of ours." Roger dismissed the matter from his mind. " I'll race you again as far as the bivvy tent. Let's make it an obstacle race, and see who can be the first dressed," he proposed.

" It's a go ! " Simon cried, immediately quickening his crawl stroke to the utmost of his power.

They reached the tent almost simultaneously, and grabbed their towels. Roger was leading in the race to dress when suddenly he stopped lacing his shoes and sniffed hard.

" I say, do I smell bacon frying ? "

" Hallo, Mrs. Hallam !   Are you an ancient

Simon gave an ecstatic sniff too.   " You do.
Some one must be up aboard the *Pride of
Lancashire*."   He took a look through the open
tent flap and chuckled.   " Oh, do look at the
boat !   Whatever are Mrs. Hallam and Marsdie
doing up there on deck ? "

Roger watched for a half minute and then
began to laugh too.

" They're doing a kind of bend with their
arms outstretched.   Up they go !   Down they
go again !   Up again !   Down again !   Whatever's possessed them ? "

Simon began to giggle.   " They're facing the

Druid priestess worshipping the sun?"

rising sun. You don't think it's some queer form of sun worship, do you?"

Roger decided to test this theory. "Hallo, Mrs. Hallam! Are you an ancient Druid priestess worshipping the sun?"

"Bend . . . Stretch! Bend . . . Stretch!" Marsdie was chanting when she heard Roger hailing them. She paused in the act of going down for the bend again. "Bother you, Roger! You would be awake and catch us at it."

"But what are you doing?" Roger persisted.

" It's the Battle of the Bulge, Roger love, and as far as I'm concerned, the Bulge seems to be winning," Mrs. Hallam answered him, laughing. " You see, Roger, I've decided I need suppleing up a bit, if I'm to keep up wi' all you young folks, so I'm doing my morning exercises, that's all."

" Mrs. Hallam, I congratulate you," Roger said, making her a sweeping bow. " You're a true sportswoman. You surprise me more and more every day with your initiative."

" Nay, Roger, as my mother used to say—" Mrs. Hallam began.

" And she was a wise woman," Marsdie could not resist putting in mischievously, then looked instantly penitent. " But do go on, please, Mrs. Hallam."

" My mother said, ' If you start being a cabbage, you can never expect to look like a butterfly ', " Mrs. Hallam trotted out triumphantly.

" So the morning exercises are by way of making you into a butterfly, eh, Mrs. Hallam?" Roger teased her.

Mrs. Hallam chuckled. " Eh, lad, I'd look a proper funny butterfly, wouldn't I ? But I'm enjoying my flitting about with you for all that. I haven't had a holiday like this for years."

" Glad to hear it, Polly," Cap'n Bill said,

appearing on the short deck of the butty boat. " Good-morning, everyone."

" Good-morning, Cap'n Bill," came in a chorus.

" My ! here are Dan and Sam too," Captain Fletcher exclaimed as the two boys appeared from below. " You are all up bright and early. You must be in a hurry to climb Rivington Pike."

" I saw Roger and Simon race across the meadow and into the water, so I thought it was high time to get up," Susan explained.

" Oh, so you two boys have been swimming already ? " the Captain asked them.

" Yes, it was great fun so bright and early," Roger said. " By the way, Cap'n Bill, there's another canal boat moored below us, down-stream."

Captain Fletcher was immediately interested. " Oh, what's she called ? "

" The *Crocus.*"

The Captain looked slightly perplexed. " That's not a name I've met with before, but there have been quite a few changes on this canal during and since the war. What was the *Crocus* carrying ? "

" We couldn't tell," Roger replied. " She was all sheeted over with tarpaulins amid-ships."

" Oh, well, it doesn't matter. I shall see

for myself when she passes us going up-stream."

"Oh, but she's not going upstream. She's headed the same way that we are going," Simon informed him.

"Perhaps the boat will turn and go about," Miss Marsden made a suggestion.

Captain Fletcher shook his head. "No, Miss Marsden. Canal boats don't turn, except at the proper places made for turning, where there's a kind of loop in the canal. The canal itself is too narrow. If the *Crocus* is headed our way, then she'll be going the same way downstream. It's strange we didn't hear her pass us last night, though."

"We were singing quite loudly, you know," Susan pointed out.

"Aye, but my ear would detect the sound of engines above all that," the Captain said.

"We thought perhaps she was moored before we came along," Simon ventured his opinion.

"Aye, lad, maybe you're right, but it was very early for cargo carriers to moor. They usually like to get alongside a wharf some-where. Still, they may be having a bit of engine trouble. Perhaps I'll take a look at them while you're all away up the Pike."

Just then Ruth called from the saloon, "Come below, everyone. Breakfast's ready."

Conversation was hastily abandoned, and there was a stampede for the saloon. Early rising had made everyone very hungry.

After breakfast Mrs. Hallam, Ruth and Marsdie made up sandwiches for the rest of the party, and, once the chores were all done, they set out for Rivington Pike, making first for Adlington village. Cap'n Bill settled himself in a nice patch of sunshine on deck, lighted his pipe and puffed away for a short time. Then he began to nod his head a little; the pipe went out and hung dangling from between his teeth, and Cap'n Bill was at peace with the world while the Brydons climbed the hill.

The Captain must have been dozing for an hour when he was awakened by a noise from round the bend of the river. It was the throb of a Diesel engine turning over quietly. Captain Fletcher started up and brushed the pipe ashes from his suit. If the people on the other barge had started their engine, then that could only mean that they intended to cast off very shortly. The Captain felt a lively curiosity to know who his neighbours on the canal could be, and what cargo they were carrying too, for very few folk on the Cut were strangers to him after his long years aboard his boat.

" I'd better be up and doing before they get

under way," he told himself, and set off at a brisk pace along the towpath.

As he rounded the bend by the belt of woodland, he expected to see the usual activity aboard, preliminary to casting off, but to his astonishment there was no one on deck at all, though the Diesel engine was pulsing quite evenly and well. The barge was still tied up to the mooring spikes.

"That's a bit queer," the Captain muttered. He reached the *Crocus* and stood by her for a minute or two, but no one appeared, and no friendly head was thrust through the hatchway.

"Hallo, there," Cap'n Bill shouted.

There was no reply, so the Captain gave a second hail, louder this time. "Hallo, there! Is there anyone aboard?"

There was a clatter of feet on the ladder, and a man put his head and shoulders through the open hatch and stared at Captain Bill. He said nothing, but stood there staring with a surly expression, and the Captain felt decidedly awkward.

"Oh, hallo," he said. "I thought you might be someone I knew, so I just gave a hail."

"Well, I'm not!" the man snapped. "What do you want?"

Captain Bill coloured a little with annoyance and indignation. Folk on the canal did not usually take each other's friendly overtures in this fashion.

"Oh, I only came to pass the time of day, being in the same line as yourself, and to ask where you were bound and what you were carrying. My boat's just a bit upstream," he told the man. This was the usual way canal boatmen started a chat, and the Captain was unaware that his curiosity could be misinterpreted as anything but a friendly interest.

The man eyed him coldly and then retorted, "What I carry and where I'm going is nobody's business but mine."

The Captain's face fell. Most canal people were only too ready to talk "shop", and often put a bit of business in each other's way. He replied rather awkwardly, "I'm sorry. No offence meant. When I heard the engine running, I expected to find you moving out; and when I saw that you weren't, I thought that maybe you might be having a bit of engine trouble, and I could help you."

The man replied quite curtly, "No help wanted," and there was nothing more the Captain could say in the face of this unfriendly attitude. He turned away and returned to the *Pride of Lancashire* feeling decidedly annoyed, and suffering from a snub he felt he had not merited. He took his seat in the sun again and lighted his pipe once more, but this time he did not find the same enjoyment in it, and he did not go to sleep again.

" All the same, I have seen that chap's face somewhere before," he said to himself reflectively. " Now, where ? "

For an hour he sat there, smoking steadily and thinking hard. Then, at the end of the time, he warmed up the dinner that Polly had left for him, ate it, washed up, and set the tea-table ready for the return of the picnic party. That done, he suddenly snapped his fingers and said, " I have it ! "

Once more he took a little walk in the direction of the *Crocus*. The engine had stopped now, and the man to whom he had spoken was sitting on the deck peeling potatoes. Captain Bill vouchsafed him only one sweeping glance, then strolled on in the direction of the bridge at Adlington, where he spent quite a bit of time leaning against the parapet and looking down into the water. Then he said to himself again, " This time I'm certain I'm right. Well, Bill lad, you'll have to do something about it." Then once more he returned to the *Pride of Lancashire*.

Not long after his arrival he heard the picnic party coming by the field path through the meadows, and he hastened to put the kettle on the oil stove. They were singing cheerfully, "We'll be coming down the mountain when we come," and he went on deck to meet them.

"Hallo! Did you have a good time up the Pike?" he asked.

"Oh, rather! It was wonderful, Cap'n Bill," they told him with enthusiasm. "What a pity you didn't come with us!"

"We'd no idea there were such lovely places in South Lancashire," Marsdie said.

"Aye, it's right bonnie country, north and south, if only you know where to look for its beauties," Cap'n Bill said proudly. "You learn to know it a lot better from a canal than by rushing through it in a bus or train."

"When we sat on top of the hill and saw all the Lancashire plain spread out before us like a map, with the rivers and the canal winding and glinting over it, and the grey-blue smoke haze rising from the towns, with the deeper blue of the sea beyond the coast, it was beautiful," Ruth said with real feeling.

"Yes, it was a bit like that bit out of the Bible, 'All the kingdoms of the world in a moment of time'," Susan said seriously.

"Aye, I reckon Rivington does give you the feeling that you're standing on top of the world," the Captain agreed. " Did you visit the Old Barn too ? " he asked.

" Yes, it's marvellous," Marsdie replied. " All those black oak beams and rafters look like trees that have grown in the place and spread their branches to the roof. It must have been a wonderful place in times past when the folk held their harvest-home dances there."

" Did you have a good time by yourself, Cap'n Bill ? " Dan asked.

" Well, Dan, kind of mixed, part agreeable and part disagreeable."

" Oh, what a pity ! Do tell us about it," Susan begged.

The Captain told them how he had heard the engine starting in the craft lying downstream, and how he had nipped along for a little good-natured investigation, and about the unfriendly reception he had had.

" That wasn't very polite of them," Susan remarked indignantly.

" No, it was jolly disconcerting when you'd only gone to pay a friendly call," Roger agreed.

" I think it was awfully rude of the man, Cap'n Bill," Ruth gave her opinion.

" If it had been me I think I should have given him a piece of my mind," Mrs. Hallam declared, giving a thump with the rolling pin to the potato cakes she was making, in a manner that boded ill for the occupant of the *Crocus*.

" It does no good, Polly," Cap'n Bill said wisely. " If there's one thing a canal teaches you, it's patience. But I've seen that chap somewhere before, and I think I know where. Never mind. Let's forget him. I've got something else to tell you. I'm afraid I've got to go to Liverpool to-morrow."

The Brydons looked at each other in consternation.

" On the *Pride of Lancashire?* " Dan asked.

" No, I'm afraid that wouldn't get me there fast enough, Dan. I shall have to go by train."

" Oh, what a pity ! What shall we all do ? Do you *have* to go, Cap'n Bill ? " were a few of the questions that sprang to everybody's lips.

" I'm afraid I must," the Captain said regretfully.

" Then would you like us all to return to Milchester, Captain Fletcher ? " Miss Marsden offered at once.

" Oh, no, no, Miss Marsden. There's no need for that. I'm only likely to be away a day at the most. I'm vexed that I've got to leave you at all, but I must."

" Shall we just stop aboard then, here, Bill ? " Mrs. Hallam asked her brother.

" I see no reason why you shouldn't. The only thing is that you might get a bit sick of staying in the same place for very long, and seeing the same bit of canal all the time. So I've been thinking there's no reason why you shouldn't take the *Pride of Lancashire* on through Wigan by yourselves."

The Brydons gasped. They had never expected the Captain to suggest this.

" Oh, Cap'n Bill, do you think we could ? " Marsdie asked with doubt.

" I don't see why you shouldn't. Roger here knows how to handle the engine very well indeed, and you're quite good as a mechanic yourself, Miss Marsden."

Marsdie blushed with pleasure at this unexpected compliment.

" And Simon's not a bad hand with the tiller," Captain Bill went on. " He could look after the butty boat with Dan and Sam to help him, and the girls to take a turn."

Dan was hopping anxiously from one leg to the other. " Oh, do let's, please, Marsdie. Do say we can. Please do. We'll all do our best."

" But what about when we come to the locks ? " Marsdie asked dubiously.

" You and Roger can manage them quite well. You've seen what's done, and you've helped to take the boat through. Besides, there's generally someone about to give a helping hand to push the balance beams, if you wait for another boat coming in the opposite direction."

Miss Marsden began to yield. " Well, if you really think we can manage it . . ." she began.

Mrs. Hallam spoke up. " There's this about it, Miss Marsden. If we find it's too much for us, we can always tie up again somewhere."

" That's right, Mrs. Hallam, we can," Roger applauded Mrs. Hallam's common-sense.

" There's a nice quiet little stretch of the canal between Appley Bridge and Parbold, three to four miles on the other side of Wigan," the Captain told them. " You could tie up there to-morrow evening, and if I've finished my business in Liverpool early, I can look for you there."

" But how would you be sure where to find us ? " Simon asked.

" Eh, Simon, on the canal, lad ! You can't lose a canal boat as easy as all that. I'll meet you somewhere between Appley Bridge and Parbold. I'll turn up, never fear."

So it was all arranged, and Miss Marsden

went to bed to dream of high towering locks with terrific balance beams, while Dan saw himself swinging the tiller in nautical fashion to the tune of a sea-shanty. As for Cap'n Bill, when he closed his eyes, he saw the face of the surly man on the *Crocus*, and he thought long and deeply about him.

Chapter Four

DAN TAKES THE PLUNGE

IN the morning after breakfast Captain Bill, attired in his neat blue suit, and looking every inch the retired captain, set off for the station at Horwich, en route for Liverpool. He had an air of grim purposefulness about him. When he had gone, the Brydons finished the usual household chores, which have to be done on a boat as much as in a house. They were rather quiet at first, and felt strangely bereft without the cheery presence of the Captain. But bit by bit the familiar tasks brought reassurance, though once Mrs. Hallam said thoughtfully, " I wonder why Bill had to go to Liverpool in such a hurry. I'm sure he wouldn't have left us like this if it wasn't something important. He isn't usually so quiet about his doings. Open as the day, Bill is. I wonder why he didn't tell us." But even Mrs. Hallam set her surmises on one side as she bustled about in the galley.

At last they were ready to quit their

moorings. Roger was in quite cheerful spirits and looking forward to being in charge of the *Pride of Lancashire*.

" Are you all ready to cast off now, Marsdie ? " he called down into the saloon.

Marsdie peered doubtfully up the hatchway. " I suppose we are, Roger. It does seem queer, though, without Captain Bill. I hope we don't make any dreadful mistakes."

" Have you and Mrs. Hallam put all the crockery safely away and lashed down the furniture in case of storm ? " Roger asked with a perfectly solemn face.

Marsdie looked instantly alarmed. " Dear me, no ! Must we do that ? " Then she saw the grin beginning to overspread Roger's face.

" Get away, Roger ! You're pulling our legs," she cried.

" There might be high seas, you know, Marsdie," Roger teased her.

Suddenly Ruth interrupted their conversation. " Listen ! What's that ? " she said.

From round the bend of the canal in the distance there came the beat of a Diesel engine. They all listened for a moment to be sure they heard aright.

" That must be our neighbours on the *Crocus* moving off downstream," Simon surmised.

Roger snapped his fingers in vexation. " Bother ! " he cried, " we shall have them ahead of us at all the locks now."

" That doesn't matter much, does it, Roger dear ? " Marsdie asked gently.

" No, not much," Roger admitted. " But we might have to wait quite a time for another boat coming upstream, to bring the water up again into the locks so it isn't wasted."

" Eh, well, we're nobbut tortoises, not hares, Roger," Mrs. Hallam said quite comfortably. " I'm sure I'm in no hurry."

Roger laughed. " At three miles an hour none of us is likely to be in a hurry, Mrs. Hallam. Well, I suppose it doesn't matter really. We're not in a hurry to unload cargo anywhere, as the canal people are. Suppose we get ready to cast off, then ? "

While Marsdie assisted Roger to oil the engine and set it gently ticking over, Simon and Dan and Sam took in the mooring-pins from the meadow, and re-coiled the mooring-ropes neatly on deck.

" You'd better take the tiller of the butty boat first, Simon," Roger directed.

Dan pulled a face at Sam. " Now it'll be *ages* before we get our turn," he muttered. Then a bright idea struck him. " It does get a bit slow sitting on deck all day while you and Simon man the boat, Roger," he called out to Roger at the engine of the *Pride of Lancashire.* " Do you think Sam and I could ride ahead on the bicycles and get the lock gates ready ? " he suggested.

" It's an idea," Roger said. " What do you think, Marsdie ? "

Miss Marsden was not quite sure whether it would be wise to let Dan have his way. He always had such a capacity for getting into mischief. Of course, Sam would be with him, with his saving grace of common-sense.

" You'd have to be awfully careful and not ride two abreast or do anything silly, you know," she warned him. " The path isn't very wide."

" Oh, we would be careful, Marsdie, we would," Dan assured her.

" The tow-path's quite flat."

" Very well, then," Marsdie agreed somewhat reluctantly.

" Give us a hand out with the bicycles, please, Simon," Dan said at once, lest Marsdie should change her mind.

Simon obliged, and the two bicycles were passed out to the tow-path.

" I'll gear up the engine now, so you two can begin riding ahead. There's no knowing how soon we might overtake you," Roger joked.

" Hurrah ! Come on, Sam ! " Dan said, mounting his bicycle at once.

" Help ! "

" Do be careful," Marsdie cautioned them.

" We'll see you all at the first lock," Sam called, mounting and riding after Dan.

Roger put the engine into gear, and its note changed a little. Marsdie was watching Dan and Sam as they approached the bend in the canal lower down.

" Oh dear ! I do wish Dan wouldn't look round to see if we were moving. He's coming terribly near to that sharp bend in the canal," Marsdie said anxiously.

Dan continued to cycle gaily on while he kept looking back over his shoulder to see if the boat had yet got under way. He waved cheerfully to Marsdie, who speechlessly signalled him to look before him. Even Sam, following behind, got a bit exasperated at the way Dan was wobbling about.

" Hi ! Look where you're going, Dan," he shouted.

It was ill luck that, at that precise moment, Dan's bicycle struck a stone in the path, causing him to wobble more erratically than ever. In attempting to right the bicycle he skidded violently towards the canal ; there were two splashes, and Dan and his bicycle disappeared beneath the water.

" Help ! " Dan cried as he went under.

Ruth and Marsdie shrieked, while Susan went deadly pale. Roger grasped the situation at once, and shouting, " Quick, Simon ! Bring that boat-hook," he dashed along the tow-path, with Simon hot behind him. As he ran, Roger flung off his jacket, intending to dive into the water to rescue Dan, but just as he reached the spot Dan came to the surface again and Sam Mitton, lying full length on the path, reached out an arm and grabbed Dan by the wrist and hung on like grim death.

" It's all right, Roger. Dan's come up again and I've got hold of him," Sam yelled. " Hold on, Dan."

" Help me out ! Help me out ! " Dan shouted. With the other hand he managed to grasp the stone edge of the canal path, but the weight of his clothes prevented him from pulling himself any farther out.

" I can't, Dan. You're too heavy. Hold on. Here comes Roger."

Roger flung himself on the bank beside Sam and grabbed both Dan's wrists.

" You get down on the canal bank beside me, Simon, and get hold of him under the left armpit, while I take him under the right. Now, Dan, you hang on to the bank with both hands while I shift my grip."

Dan and Sam did as they were directed, and Roger got a good hold of Dan by his shoulders.

" Now, Sam, you sit on my legs while I haul

at him," Roger ordered. "Susan, you sit on Simon's. We don't want him to pull us all in. Now, Simon, let us see if we can lock our grip together right across Dan's chest, holding under opposite armpits."

Very cautiously they shifted their grips again until they had got Dan between their arms.

"Now, *heave!*" Roger cried.

Together they heaved, and Dan pulled his hardest on the edge of the bank too. They got his chest level with the side of the canal, and, once he was able to get his elbows on to the tow-path, it was an easy matter after that for him to get a knee up, and, supported by Simon and Roger, partly to scramble out himself, and partly to be pulled out.

"Here he comes!" Roger cried, and in a second more Dan's soaking dripping figure was on the tow-path beside them.

"Oh, thank goodness you've pulled him out, Roger," Marsdie cried, almost weeping with relief.

"Oh, I've swallowed half the canal," Dan spluttered.

Roger felt angry with Dan for causing this unfortunate adventure by his carelessness just at the outset of their journey by themselves without Captain Bill.

"You're a silly little donkey, Dan, cycling

along and not looking where you were going,"
he scolded.

" It was a big stone in the path that set me
skidding," Dan began to explain, shivering,
partly with the chill of the water and partly
with the fright he had had. Marsdie seized hold
of him by the arm and began to run him back
along the towpath to the *Pride of Lancashire*.

" No time for scolding and explanations
now, either of you," she called back to Roger
over her shoulder.   " The thing to do is to get
Dan back on the boat and strip those wet
things off and get him into dry clothes."

" I'll come and help him to rub down," Sam
volunteered.

" I'll run ahead and make a hot drink for
him," Ruth said.

By this time Mrs. Hallam had come up to
them.   She seized Dan's other arm, and only
his soaking state prevented her from folding
him to her bosom.

" Eh, Dan love, come on, my precious lamb.
Thank goodness Sam managed to grab hold
of you ! "

" Well, Simon, we'd better try to get the
bike out that Mrs. Hallam's precious lamb
rode into the water," Roger said grimly.
" Come on, give me the boat-hook."

" It's going to be something of a juggling
trick.   I'd better get the boat-hook belonging

to the butty boat, too," Simon decided. He ran back and returned in a minute. " Here we are. I can't even *see* the bike, Dan's churned up the mud so much."

" It won't have floated away, anyhow. He went in right opposite this tree," Roger pointed out. " Dip the boat-hook in and try to grapple the bike."

Their first cast brought no result.

" Perhaps if one of us put on a bathing costume and *dived* for it . . ." Simon was beginning to suggest.

" And come up like a mud pie ! No, thank you ! " Roger said emphatically. " No, let's have another go with the boat-hooks."

They poked about once more among the mud at the bottom of the canal.

" I've got hold of *something*," Simon announced. " I don't know whether it's the bike or not, but it doesn't feel like it." He heaved mightily on the end of his boat-hook, and Roger stood ready to assist with his. A dark object broke the surface of the water. " It's coming up ! " Roger cried. " No, it's not the bike. It's a sack with something heavy in it."

There was a distinct clank of metal from the sack.

" That sounds like iron or something heavy," Simon said.

Roger got his boat-hook into the sack and heaved too. Soon they had it on the tow-path beside them. It was a sack tied up with a rope at the top. Roger cut the rope with his jack-knife.

" Now, let's have a look at this treasure of the deep," he said, and he tipped out the contents of the sack on to the tow-path. " It looks like some chunks of old metal," he added, regarding his find with a mystified air.

Simon was turning over the pieces of metal too. He examined one of the heavier pieces with a thoughtful expression. " This is a bit like one of the stamping presses I've seen at some exhibition, only it's smaller than the one there. And this is like a small metal lathe, too." He picked up some long narrow shiny pieces of metal.

" But what are these ? "

" They look like short bars or rails," Roger said. " I wonder where they came from ? "

" They're queer things to find in a sack in the canal," Simon commented. " I suppose they must have rolled off some barge."

" Hardly *rolled*," Roger said. " They're far too heavy for that, though they may have been accidentally pushed overboard when some heavier piece of cargo was being taken off."

" But what heavy piece of cargo would be

taken off just at this place ? " Simon objected. " There's no wharf nearer than Adlington, more than a mile away, and there's not even a farm cart road comes down to the water here, so no piece of farm machinery would be put off at this spot, either."

" It's a queer thing," Roger agreed. " Anyway, these things have come out of the canal. That's a fact. Perhaps some workman dropped his tools in and had nothing with him to fish them out again."

" Perhaps. They can't have been in the canal long. The sack looks as good as new," Simon pointed out.

" It's a strange business, but I suppose it's just one of those mysteries we shall never solve." Roger gave it up.

" What shall we do with them ? " Simon asked.

" I don't know. Perhaps we'd better take them aboard and wait till Cap'n Bill gets back to us this evening. He'll know what to do with them, sure enough," Roger decided.

Simon laughed. " He'll probably know just who has dropped them. He knows nearly everyone on this canal."

Roger nodded. " And now we've got that bicycle to recover. Let's both grapple with the boat-hooks, Simon."

They both poked away among the mud, in

and around the spot where Dan had fallen in, for a minute or two without result, then Simon shifted the area of his operations by another yard, and immediately cried out, " Here it is ! I can feel the wheel."

Roger also grappled for it, and exclaimed, " So can I. If you can get your boat-hook through the frame of the bicycle, perhaps I can get mine round the handlebars."

Gently they worked round with the boat-hooks till Roger decided they had got a sufficient grip, then cautiously, very cautiously indeed, they began to bring them up gently, keeping level with each other.

" It's coming up," Simon said triumphantly. " Pull in towards the side now, Roger."

The bicycle broke the surface, and inch by inch they drew it nearer to the side. When it was within gripping distance Roger said, " Can you hold the two poles steady, Simon, while I lie on the path and lean forward and grip the handlebars ? "

" Yes, I'll try," Simon agreed, " but it's going to be a bit of a task even then."

" I know. That's why I want to get a grip of it first and pass this rope round it so we don't lose it again."

Simon supported the weight of the bicycle on the two boat-hooks, while Roger wriggled half over the canal and fixed a rope round the handlebars and frame. Susan had appeared round the bend of the canal again to see if they had succeeded in rescuing the bicycle, and Roger quickly pressed her into service.

" Here, Susan. You take the end of this rope and give it a turn or two round that tree while Simon and I hold the bicycle. Whatever you do, don't let go of that rope."

Susan obeyed, and in a trice the tree was taking the strain of the rope.

" Stay just where you are and hang on to the end of it," Roger instructed her. Slowly he rose to his knees, taking in what small slack there was on the rope as he stood up.

" Now, you heave with the boat-hooks and I'll pull," he told Simon.

Simon heaved and Roger pulled, and in a moment or two the bicycle was clear of the water and lying on the tow-path beside them.

" Thank goodness we've got that out," Roger said, just as Miss Marsden joined them too.

" Well done, Roger ! I thought it was gone for good," Marsdie declared.

" How's Dan ? " Roger asked as he coiled up the rope again.

" Clean and dry once more. I've made him lie down in his bunk for an hour or two, just in case he has had any slight shock, and Ruth has given him some hot milk to drink—and

Sam too, bless him ! Dan doesn't seem any the worse for the ducking, but his big worry is to know whether you've got his bicycle out, so I said I'd come along and see how you were doing with it."

" You can set his mind at rest then, Marsdie, but really he is a holy terror for getting into scrapes. He deserves a jolly good scolding along with that hot milk."

" What's this ? " Marsdie said, looking with surprise at the wet sack and its contents, which lay tumbled on the path.

" Some old junk or other that we've pulled out of the canal."

" Oh, Roger, is it anything valuable ? " Susan asked.

Roger shook his head. " No, I don't think so. They're just discarded tools and bits of metal, I imagine. We'll take them aboard with us and let Cap'n Bill have a look at them to-night. He might have an idea who has lost them."

" Right. You take the sack, Roger, and I'll wheel the bicycle," Simon suggested. " It doesn't seem any the worse for its swim in the canal, but it will need wiping down and oiling in every part to prevent rust."

" And when we've done that, let's hope we'll be able to get under way at last. It's nearly ten o'clock, and we've a number of

95

locks between here and Wigan, and you can't hurry a canal boat, you know," Roger said, looking a little worried.

When they reached the *Pride of Lancashire*, Simon asked Roger where he thought they had better put the sack.

" In the hold of the butty boat ? " Roger said at first, then thought again. " No, we might trip over it when we were getting bicycles or the tent out some time. We'd better store it forrad under Dan's bunk. There's a space underneath."

" Good idea ! " Simon paused in the act of assisting Roger with the sack. " Listen, Roger. I had an awfully strange feeling when we were examining that sack and getting the bicycle out that someone was watching us all the time."

" Oh ! Where ? " Roger asked.

" In that plantation of trees behind us."

" Did you actually see anyone ? "

Simon shook his head. " No, though there were lots of bushes behind which someone might have been concealed. Once I *thought* I saw the bushes move as though someone had parted the branches, but I couldn't be sure."

" Imagination, Simon ? Though it's usually Susan who hears and sees things that no one else does," Roger said.

" Quite likely it was imagination," Simon conceded.

" Come on, then. You take the tiller of the butty boat, and I'll go and start the engine once more with Marsdie's help," Roger urged. " If we don't get a move on, we'll never be through those locks near Wigan. I should think by now that other boat, the *Crocus*, will be miles ahead."

It was getting well on in the afternoon when, after successfully negotiating the Wigan Top Lock above Rose Bridge, the *Pride of Lancashire* began to slide between the smoke-begrimed houses that marked the eastern approaches to Wigan. Susan regarded the mills and blackened chimneys of this busy mining and cotton-weaving town with some disfavour, till she thought of what Captain Bill had said to them about there being even a strange grim beauty in the towns.

" I suppose there are some nice clean parts of Wigan," she said to Marsdie a little doubtfully.

" Certain to be, Susan," Marsdie replied cheerfully. " At any rate I mean to explore the town and see for myself. I have some shopping to do, if you people are to get anything to eat."

In a short time they were too busy negotiating the Wigan Bottom Lock to take much stock of their surroundings, for everyone had to lend a hand to turn the windlass and work the balance beam while Roger and Simon successfully piloted the *Pride of Lancashire* and her attendant butty boat through the locks. At last the lock gates were closed behind them, and not long afterwards they found themselves lying alongside the old Wigan Wharf in Wallgate. Miss Marsden stared around her where the giant cotton mills, like Trencherfield Mill, raised their many-windowed walls.

" So this is Wigan," she said, and gave something like a sign of relief to think that they had at last arrived. " We didn't manage those two locks so badly after all, *mes enfants*," she declared with satisfaction.

" Careful, Marsdie ! " Roger warned her. " Pride goes before a fall, you know. We've still four or five locks to get through before we can tie up for the night beyond Appley Bridge."

" Good gracious ! " Marsdie exclaimed. " Why, canal locks round Wigan are as plentiful as blackberries on a bush ! I wonder if Captain Fletcher remembered there were quite so many when he blithely let us start out adventuring on our own ? "

Mrs. Hallam gave a sniff. " If you ask me, Bill wanted to get off on his own to Liverpool for some mysterious reason, and he was quite pleased to let us have the job."

Mrs. Hallam was secretly a little put out that her brother had not told her why he was going to Liverpool in such a hurry.

" Oh, come, Mrs. Hallam," Roger rallied her. " You know quite well you're *enjoying* these locks. Look at the way you stood on deck at the last one and issued orders just like an Admiral of the Fleet. All you want is a cocked hat and a bit of gold braid to be complete."

" Now, now, Roger," Mrs. Hallam cautioned him with a shake of her fist. " All the same, Miss Marsden, I thought we didn't give a bad account of ourselves."

" Of course we were helped quite a bit," Marsdie admitted. " Those miners walking along the tow-path were jolly kind the way they helped us to work the locks and push the beam."

" Privately I thought it was Mrs. Hallam's weight on the balance beam that made all the difference whether the lock gates closed or didn't," Roger remarked with an innocent air.

Mrs. Hallam rather enjoyed Roger's teasing, and merely replied, " Now, Roger, none of your sauce."

" But I do think Wigan folk are kind, all the same," Ruth said. " Look at that woman at the cottage who ran out to ask if we needed any hot water or milk."

" Yes, Wigan folk are kind," Roger agreed, " though she probably thought we looked like a Sunday School picnic.   Well, does everyone want to tie up here at Wigan Wharf ? "

" Oh, yes," Marsdie said promptly.   " Mrs. Hallam and I have some shopping to do."

" I'd like to see if there's anything of historic interest in the town," Simon said. Simon was deeply interested in old buildings and everything connected with the bygone life of the people, and Miss Marsden shared this interest with him.

" There's sure to be, Simon," Marsdie said. " I admit we've come through a rather grimy industrial part of the town, but often the centre of these busy towns is awfully nice."

" Like people with grim exteriors but kind hearts, eh, Marsdie ? " Roger said.   " Then we'll tie up here and visit the town."

Just then a wharfman approached them.

" I suppose this is the right place to leave our boat if we want to go ashore and see Wigan ? " Roger asked him.

" Aye, lad, this is Wigan Pier," the man told him with a twinkle in his eye.   " Are you coming ashore to hear the band ? "

" Why, is there one ? " Dan asked innocently, for once completely taken in.

When the others had done laughing Simon asked, " Is there any fine old building of historic interest in the town ?   Any castle ? "

" No, there's no castle, but there's a grand old church, the Parish Church," the wharfman said promptly, with quite a degree of pride. " A fine old tower it's got, too, dating back to Norman times."

" I'd like to see that," Simon declared.

" And are there any good shops ? " Marsdie asked.

" Wigan shops are the best in the world, ma'am," the wharfman declared. " And you've come on a grand day for shopping. It's Friday—Market Day in Wigan. Just you take a walk round Wigan Market Square and you'll find all the stalls set up, wi' fruit and vegetables of every kind you want and right cheap.   It's a sight for sore eyes."

" Then we mustn't miss it," Marsdie said gaily.

" I suppose it will be all right to leave the boats here with no one on them ? " Roger asked the wharfman.

" If you can lock up the cabins, lad, they'll be all right.   I shall be here all afternoon, and I'll keep an eye on the boats to see that no one walks off wi' one," the wharfman offered jokingly.

" What about Dog Jonathan ? " Dan asked.

" Is that your dog ? Have you got a lead for him ? "

" No. You forgot to hide Jonathan's lead when you hid him in the car to bring him on this trip, Dan," Ruth reminded him.

" Then I should leave the little dog aboard in a cabin," the wharfman said promptly. " There'll be crowds of folk at the market. You might lose him there."

" That would be awkward," Marsdie agreed. " Perhaps it would be better to leave him in the cabin this time, Dan, and give him a scamper when we come to green fields again."

" All right," Dan agreed rather reluctantly. " We shan't be long, Jonathan, old man. I'll bring you back some dog biscuits and a nice bone."

" Come on, then, folks," Mrs. Hallam said, locking the doors of the cabins behind her and putting the keys in her capacious handbag.

They went ashore and up the street, under the railway bridge, to the steady rise of Wallgate into the centre of the town. Suddenly, as they passed the Post Office, Simon caught a glimpse of the Parish Church behind some shops and offices.

" There it is ! " he cried in some excitement. " There's the Parish Church with its Norman tower. Oh, Marsdie, can we go there first ? "

Marsdie hesitated. " Well, I'd like to get

to the market before all the best things are sold, Simon."

" Let's split up the party, then," Roger suggested. " How would it be if I and Simon and Dan and Sam take a look at the Parish Church while you ladies do the shopping ? "

" Excellent, Roger," Marsdie agreed. "After all, if eight of us stood in front of a stall in the market to buy tomatoes, the rest of the population of Wigan wouldn't stand much of a chance. I think we'd better arrange to meet at the wharf again in about an hour and a half."

" Very well," Roger said, looking at his wrist-watch. " We'll be there."

Mrs. Hallam, Marsdie and the two girls hurried away down Market Street, while the others made a bee-line through the old flagged churchyard to the church.

After the shopping was done, Marsdie and Mrs. Hallam were returning to the wharf by way of Wallgate, laden with baskets and parcels, when there was a sound of running feet behind them as the four boys tried to catch up.

" Just in time," Roger said, seizing the biggest basket from Mrs. Hallam and the largest parcel from Marsdie. " You look just like two Christmas trees, hung about with mysterious knobby packages."

" Well, how did you like Wigan ? " Simon asked them.

" Do you know, I think Wigan is an awfully nice town after all," Susan admitted.

" I like the way the town seems to cluster round the old Parish Church, as though all the roads led to it," Simon said.

" I expect they did once, Simon," Marsdie agreed. " Mrs. Hallam and I liked that great paved Market Square with all the farmers' stalls set out on it, piled with apples and pears and plums and tomatoes."

" Yes, and with cabbages and sticks of celery, beetroot and beans," Ruth chanted. " My shopping bag's just laden. We shan't need to do any more shopping till we reach Liverpool, I think."

" I enjoyed the way the stall-holders all shouted their wares at you. I just couldn't resist it when one of them yelled, ' 'Ere y'are, luv, three pound o' beetroot for elevenpence h'penny ! Beet that yer can't beat ! ' " Marsdie laughed.

Ruth looked sideways at Marsdie. " Three pounds of beetroot, Marsdie ! But how are we going to get through all that ? "

Marsdie looked rather conscience-stricken.

" Never you mind, Miss Marsden. A salad or two and a bit pickled, and it'll soon be gone," Mrs. Hallam said comfortably.

" Besides, I saved a whole ha'penny by taking the three pounds, remember," Marsdie pointed out with pride.

" I loved all those masses and masses of flowers on the flower stalls," Susan said. " I thought the whole market was full of colour."

" Did you find anything interesting in the church, Simon ? " Marsdie asked.

" Oh, yes. There was a crusader's tomb in the church, with a stone knight in armour upon it. He was Sir William Bradshaigh, and beside him there was another stone figure of his wife, dressed in a long flowing robe like ladies wore about the early fourteenth century. She was Lady Mabel Bradshaigh."

" Oh, we can tell you all about Lady Mabel, can't we, Sam ? " Dan said unexpectedly.

" Aye. Dan and I climbed the hill out of the town on the other side, and we came to a very old wayside cross set in a school garden."

" Go on. This is interesting," Simon urged them.

" So we asked a policeman what it was, and he told us it was ' Mab's Cross ', short for the Lady Mabel, you know," Dan told them.

" Aye. Sir William went away on a crusade and word came back to Haigh Hall that he was killed," Sam took up the story. " So, to keep her home for her children, Lady Mabel married a wicked knight who took her lands from her."

" But Sir William wasn't killed at all, and he came back and slew the wicked knight, and he and Lady Mabel lived happily at Haigh Hall afterwards," Dan finished the story.

" Except that Lady Mabel was very sorry she married the wicked knight while her own husband was still alive, so once a year she walked barefoot from Haigh to Mab's Cross to show how sorry she was," Sam added.

" Well, just imagine that ! " Mrs. Hallam said. " The poor soul ! Eh, I'd never have thought Wigan was as old as that."

All this time they had been making their way to the wharf.

" Here we are at the *Pride of Lancashire* again," Roger said.

The wharfman was standing by their boat, and greeted them cheerfully. " Well, did you enjoy your visit into the town ? "

" Yes, we did. It's a jolly nice town. What splendid shops ! Wigan's very interesting," came from them all in a chorus.

" Aye, it was proper champion," Sam added the final word of praise.

The wharfman looked very pleased. "That's good. I'm glad you enjoyed yourselves. Your boat belongs to Cap'n Bill Fletcher, doesn't it ? "

" Yes, he's my brother," Mrs. Hallam said proudly.

" I didn't recognize the boat at first. She's done up so smart. I've kept my eye on her all right, but maybe it's as well you left your dog aboard."

" Why ? " Roger asked quickly.

" There was a queer-looking customer tried to step aboard her, but the dog heard him and barked loudly at him from the cabin, and that brought me along pretty quick. The chap backed away then, and said he was just kind of interested in the boat, and he thought he might know the folk aboard," the wharfman told him.

" Oh ! " Miss Marsden said, very surprised.

" I asked him what his name was and whether he'd like to leave a message for you, and said that you were likely to be back any minute," the wharfman continued.

" And did he leave a message ? " Miss Marsden asked.

" No, ma'am. He said it didn't matter and that perhaps he'd be back soon. I thought he looked a bit shady. There are plenty of sneak-thieves about the country to-day. I'd keep the cabin locked and your eyes open if you go ashore anywhere else," the wharfman cautioned them.

" Thanks. We will. It was jolly decent of

you to look after our boat," Roger thanked him.

" You're welcome," the man replied in his genial Lancashire fashion.

When Mrs. Hallam opened the cabin door, Jonathan welcomed them with joyous barking and many leaps into the air.

" Hallo, Dog Jonathan ! I've got a whacking great bone for you," Marsdie said, taking a parcel from the basket.

" You know, it's a jolly good thing I did bring Jonathan with us. He certainly looked after the boats while we were away, and kept tramps from stealing our things," Dan pointed out.

" As things have turned out, that's true," Roger admitted.

" I expect it's really a coincidence, Roger, but when we were coming back to the boat, I thought we met one of the men off that canal boat at Adlington. You know—the *Crocus*," Simon said to Roger in a quiet voice.

" Are you sure ? " Roger asked sharply.

" Yes, pretty sure, though I couldn't be absolutely certain, but I thought it was the same face I saw for a moment at the port-hole when we were swimming. Of course, I only had a glimpse."

" It might possibly be someone who was a bit like him ? " Roger surmised.

" Possibly," Simon admitted. " Though this man stared rather hard at us."

" Maybe we're imagining things, but all the same we'd better keep our eyes open," Roger decided. " I wouldn't like anything to happen to the *Pride of Lancashire* while it was in our charge, particularly when Cap'n Bill trusted us so decently. Well, we'd better be moving again. We've quite a few locks to negotiate before we tie up at our moorings for the night with Appley Bridge behind us."

Chapter Five

ATTACK AT NIGHTFALL

IT was already past six o'clock when the *Pride of Lancashire* reached Appley Lock, half a mile further on from the pretty little village of Appley Bridge.

" Cheers ! " Roger cried. " This is the very last lock before we tie up for the night. Get ready to do your stuff."

As they came up to the lock they found they were in luck. The water was in the top lock and the gates were open. That meant there need be no long wait.

" Hurrah ! I can guide the boat right in," Roger said with satisfaction. " All you will have to do will be to close the top gates behind me and wind open the sluices on the lower gates."

" Come on, Mrs. Hallam. Come on, *mes enfants*," Marsdie rallied her forces. " More physical jerks for you all while we push the balance beam."

" Eh, I'll be as thin as a needle soon," Mrs.

Hallam declared, placing her weight at a strategic point on the beam.

" Sing a sea-shanty, everyone. It does help," Marsdie directed.

Sam started, " Where have ye been all the day, Billy Boy, Billy Boy ? " and they all pushed with a right good will to the rhythm of the song.

" Go on. You're doing splendidly," Roger encouraged them from the boat.

The great doors drifted together, and the Brydons were ready to start opening the sluices in the lower lock gates.

" You can get busy on the winding handle and open the sluices to let the level of the water down in the lock now, Marsdie," Roger directed.

" Willingly," Marsdie said. " Pass me the windlass, Roger."

Roger looked in the place where the windlass was usually kept, but it was not there.

" It's not here. Where did you put it, Marsdie ? " he called.

" I thought it was beside the engine, but I must have been mistaken. See if I've carried it into the cabin, Ruth."

Ruth took a look, but the windlass was not there. " No, it's nowhere there, and it's a bit big for you to conceal inside the teapot, Marsdie."

" Oh dear ! What can I have done with it ? " Marsdie cried, distracted.

A frantic hunt ensued aboard both the *Pride of Lancashire* and the butty boat, but nowhere could they find the missing windlass.

" It looks as though we're going to have to make our home in this lock for the night," Roger exclaimed. " Here we are, and here we're stuck."

" Are you sure you brought the windlass away from the last lock—the Dean Lock, wasn't it ? " Ruth asked.

Marsdie clapped her hands to her head. " Oh, Ruth, now I remember ! I left it on the winding gear there. Oh, what shall we do ? "

The Brydons looked from one to another in consternation.

" Goodness, what a mess ! " Roger voiced everyone's thoughts. " Here we shall have to stick until we get that winding handle, or some other barge comes upstream and we can borrow one."

" We might wait for an hour or more for someone coming along. It's getting towards evening," Simon pointed out. " Listen. *I'll* cycle back to Dean Lock and get the windlass. It's less than a couple of miles away. I'll be there and back in under half an hour, easily."

Simon lifted a bicycle out on to the tow-path.

"Oh, do be careful, Simon," Marsdie warned him, thinking of Dan's escapade.

Simon laughed. "Don't worry, Marsdie. I shan't try to become a submarine like Dan did."

He mounted and rode away quite gaily. "Shan't be long!" he called over his shoulder.

Marsdie looked very penitent. "I am sorry, Roger," she said. "I've really blotted my copybook this time, and I thought I was getting so frightfully clever at handling this barge and working the locks. You warned me at Wigan that pride went before a fall, and how true it has been."

"Never mind, Marsdie. All we've got to do is to sit and wait. It's not a bad spot to have to sit and wait at, anyway," Roger consoled Marsdie.

Within ten minutes Susan spied Simon returning, cycling quickly but carefully.

"Here's Simon already!" she cried. "He has been quick."

Simon, breathless and red in the face, dismounted. In his hand was the missing windlass.

"Eh, Simon love, you haven't been long," Mrs. Hallam hailed him. "You can't have been there and back in that short time."

"As your mother used to say, and she was a wise woman, 'Necessity gives you wings'," Simon teased Mrs. Hallam. "Here's the windlass, Marsdie."

"You have been quick! Had I really left it at the Dean Lock, Simon?"

"Well, Marsdie, you had, but our friend, the kindly lock-keeper, had found it there when another boat was coming up, and after he'd let the boat through, he came on his cycle to bring it to us and I met him half-way," Simon explained.

"How jolly decent of him," Roger said.

"Yes, wasn't it? He said he knew we'd be stuck at this lock till someone turned up with a winding handle. He'd have asked the chaps on the following boat to bring it to us, but they said they weren't coming so far to-night."

Roger thought that Simon gave them the last little piece of information in a rather strange tone of voice.

"Did you see what the boat was?" he asked casually.

"Yes, I saw it in the distance, and, to make sure, I asked the lock-keeper too," Simon said in a rather quiet voice that the others, busy already with the windlass, could not hear.

"To make sure?" Roger repeated, rather surprised.

" Yes. It was the *Crocus*, the boat belonging to that surly man who was so rude to Captain Bill. You know, the one that was moored below us near Adlington yesterday," Simon told him.

Roger looked puzzled. " *Below*, and they left before we did, and now they're above us on the canal and *behind* us ! How could that happen ? "

" We must have passed them somewhere," Simon said.

" That's plain enough. But where ? Surely we should have noticed them on the canal ? "

" There's one place where they might have waited and we might have passed them without noticing them," Simon said slowly.

" Where ? "

" At the Wharf in Wigan where we tied up. The *Crocus* might have been tied up already in another part of the wharf basin. There's a kind of loop there—a sort of harbour, almost."

" Gosh ! I believe you're right. They might have been moored higher up in the basin than we were."

" Exactly," Simon said.

He and Roger looked at each other. The same thought came into both their minds, and they read it in each other's eyes. Was the mysterious visitor to the *Pride of Lancashire*, while they were all ashore in Wigan, none other than one of the men from the *Crocus*?

"Of course, it's probably just a coincidence," Simon meditated.

"Probably. After all, the *Crocus* has to move up and down the canal just as we do. Only I wish we had more friendly neighbours."

"Another thing," Simon added, this time wrinkling his brows more thoughtfully still, "they had asked the lock-keeper at Dean Lock if we'd gone through."

"They did, did they?"

"Yes, and he told them we had and that we intended mooring farther down beyond Appley Lock. You remember we happened to tell the lock-keeper that when we were chatting to him."

"Mm." Roger looked a little concerned. "Of course, everybody on the canal asks everybody else who is in front or who is behind, only they say 'below' or 'above'. Cap'n Bill always asks that."

"That is so," Simon agreed. "Though the men on the *Crocus* were not quite so chatty and sociable when Cap'n Bill went to talk to them."

"I know. Still, it's probably nothing more or less than a coincidence that they're moored not very far from us again. All the same, I don't think we'd better leave the boat unattended this evening if we decide to take a walk. There might be sneak-thieves aboard the *Crocus*."

" You're right. The wharfman at Wigan did warn us," Simon concurred.

They said no more, for by now Miss Marsden and the others had the lock sluices fully opened, and the water was sinking in the lock, so Roger and Simon bent their energies to manœuvring the *Pride of Lancashire* and her attendant butty boat out of the lock once more, and in lending a hand to close the lock gates behind them.

" Anyway, if the *Crocus* comes through that lock we shall know, as she's bound to pass us if we moor a few hundred yards lower down as we arranged with Cap'n Bill," Roger told Simon.

After they had moored the boat and made all secure for the night Miss Marsden asked the Brydons, " What are you going to do with yourselves this evening ? "

" I should like a walk to stretch my legs," Ruth declared. Ruth had an active nature and always liked to be busy doing something. When there was no cooking to be done, then she liked to occupy herself with some handwork or other employment in or out of doors.

" We did promise to take Jonathan for a run," Dan reminded them.

" I'd like to go to the top of that funny-looking little hill that seems to be crowned with a *bottle ?* " Susan said, pointing to a hill about a mile away.

" So it is ! It's just like a stone bottle on the top of it," Simon chuckled.

" It'll be one of the old beacon hills round-about, no doubt, where bonfires were lit in times of war during the olden days," Marsdie told them. " Probably there was a bonfire there in Queen Elizabeth's day to warn the people that the Spanish Armada had been sighted approaching the shores."

" I remember folk around used to call it Parbold Bottle," Mrs. Hallam informed them.

" Come on, then, let's go," Dan urged them.

Roger and Simon hesitated, looking at each other, unwilling to alarm the others by suggesting that it might be unwise to leave the boat unattended ; before they had time to speak, Miss Marsden voiced their thoughts.

" Perhaps we shouldn't all go, as Cap'n Bill left the boat in our charge."

" I'll stay then, Marsdie," Roger offered at once.

" I'll keep Roger company," Simon said promptly, but Marsdie shook her head.

" No, *I'll* stay," she said quite firmly, " and then I can have supper ready for you when you come back."

" No, no ! " the Brydons protested.

" I'd like to, though," Marsdie persisted. " It's really quite selfish of me, because I bought a very interesting book in Wigan, and I'm just dying for quiet to read it."

Dan looked at her with wide-open eyes. " I really believe Marsdie means it," he said.

" I think I'll stay as well and put my feet up and lose myself for a bit," Mrs. Hallam declared comfortably. " Rivington Pike yesterday and then tramping round Wigan to-day is quite enough for my poor old feet."

" Why not try paddling in the canal, Mrs. Hallam ? That might do them good," Roger advised her with a far too innocent air.

" Go on, Roger ! I haven't brought a diving suit with me, so you won't have me on toast, nor yet on a mud bank in the canal either," Mrs. Hallam retorted merrily, not to be taken in.

" Well, if you and Mrs. Hallam really don't mind being the ' watches ' aboard, Marsdie—" Roger began.

" Not a bit. If you're going to Parbold Bottle before it gets dark, you'd better set off at once," Marsdie advised them.

" Yes, do come along, everyone. Jonathan's dying for his scamper," Dan urged them.

They set off for the crossing which would take them over the railway, some little distance away, for the railway lay between them and the hill. As they went, they tried to keep the Bottle on the skyline as a landmark. Jonathan scampered in front of them, ever and again rushing back just to make sure that they were coming, thoroughly pleased with himself and them.

Aboard the barge, Mrs. Hallam settled herself comfortably on the divan and closed her eyes. Miss Marsden unwrapped her book from the parcel and was soon deep in its pages. There was no sound save the regular monotonous tick of the clock. Anyone passing the boat might easily have assumed that there was no one aboard at all. The shadows began to lengthen, and it grew dusky in the cabin. Miss Marsden set down her book and closed her eyes for a few minutes, while from the divan came the gentle sounds of Mrs. Hallam's comfortable slumber.

It must have been half-an-hour later that Miss Marsden awoke with a start as though some unexpected noise had disturbed her. Mrs. Hallam started too, and rubbed her eyes.

" Eh, I've had a proper nice forty winks,"

she declared. " My, but it's going dark, isn't it ? "

" Yes, I must have been asleep too," Miss Marsden confessed. " It's time we lit the lamps."

" I'd better be seeing to the supper," Mrs. Hallam said, and put one leg from the divan to the floor, but her progress was halted by Miss Marsden holding up a finger and saying, " Ssh ! Listen ! Is that someone moving about on the butty boat ? "

Both listened, not moving. There was undoubtedly someone stirring about on the butty boat. Miss Marsden got up from her chair and went to the little ladder leading from the cabin and, going up a step or two, thrust her head above the deck level. She caught a glimpse of a flash from a torch and a shadowy figure.

" Has one of the children come back ? " Mrs. Hallam asked in a low voice, though she too thought it queer that, if the children had returned, they had failed to hail them in their usual cheery fashion.

" I'm going aboard the butty boat to find out," Marsdie answered her quietly.

" I'll come with you, then," Mrs. Hallam declared stoutly.

Just as Miss Marsden was about to step from the tow-path on to the butty boat, a man emerged from the cabin with a sack on his back.

" Here ! What are you doing on that boat ? " Marsdie shouted sharply.

" Get out of my way ! " the man cried, elbowing Miss Marsden aside.

" Put that sack down at once," Miss Marsden ordered him valiantly, laying a hand on the sack.

" Get out of my way, I tell you," the man shouted at her.

" Give me that sack," Miss Marsden said, clenching her teeth in determination, and taking a better grip on the sack.

" Let go, missus, or I'll land you one as 'll knock you into the canal," the man threatened her.

" I shan't ! " Miss Marsden cried defiantly.

The man aimed a brutal blow at her face, thinking to make her lose her hold on the sack, but the blow fell short and merely grazed her shoulder. Her assailant had reckoned without Mrs. Hallam, who, barge pole in hand, had advanced to the attack and dealt him a shrewd blow across the shins with it.

" You wait ! I'll——" the man was bereft of words with pain and temper.

Suddenly he snatched the sack from Miss Marsden's detaining grip and tried to jump ashore, but out of the darkness came an angry

" Stop thief !   Stop him, Jonathan ! "

bark and a small black and white fury launched
itself to the attack on him. It was Dog
Jonathan.

"Stop thief ! Stop him, Jonathan ! At
him ! " Miss Marsden cried wildly.

"Catch him, Jonathan ! Catch him ! "
came in Ruth's voice from the tow-path.

Jonathan sprang and snapped and sprang
and snapped again. The man let loose a
volley of curses and leaped ashore, fighting off
the dog. There was a splash in the water as
the sack fell from his shoulder into the
canal.

"Jonathan's bitten him! Good lad, Jonathan!" Mrs. Hallam cried.

The man found the combination of three determined people and a dog too much for him, especially when Mrs. Hallam advanced furiously to the attack once more with the barge pole. He turned tail and fled up the tow-path. When he was out of reach of the flailing weapon, he called back angrily to them, "Don't you think I've finished with you. I'll be back, you'll soon find out, and others with me." Then he disappeared into the darkness.

"Oh, Marsdie, are you all right?" Ruth cried.

"Yes, quite all right, but what happened to the sack?" Marsdie said instantly.

"I saw it fall from the end of the butty boat, and then I heard a splash," Ruth said. "Oh, Marsdie, at first I thought it was you whom that ruffian had knocked into the water."

"It was a very lucky thing you came up with Jonathan just when you did, Ruth," Mrs. Hallam said thankfully. "It was grand the way Jonathan flew at that man. Good little dog!" She patted Jonathan's head.

"I decided I'd hurry on ahead of the others with Jonathan, so that I could help to get the supper ready," Ruth said. "How thankful I am that I did."

"Certainly Jonathan helped to save the situation. I wish that sack hadn't fallen into the water. It's the one Roger and Simon fished out of the canal this morning. I wonder if we could get it out again?" Marsdie said, peering into the dark depths of the canal at the stern of the butty boat.

"There's something very queer about that sack if the man would go to such lengths to get it," Ruth declared. "I think we should try to get it out and hand it to the police."

"Right! You take one boat-hook and I'll take the other. You keep a watch, Ruth, in case that man comes back," Mrs. Hallam said.

Mrs. Hallam and Miss Marsden prodded about with the long boat-hooks till they had located the sack again at the stern of the butty boat.

"I've got hold of something, Miss Marsden," Mrs. Hallam cried. "Plunge your boat-hook in here beside mine."

"Yes, I've hooked something too," Miss Marsden announced. "Let's try to lift it gently, Mrs. Hallam. We don't want it to drop off again."

"Here it comes!" Mrs. Hallam cried triumphantly as the sack appeared above the water. "It's the sack, right enough."

" Can you get a grip on it, Ruth ? " Marsdie asked. " Mind you don't overbalance."

Ruth reached out and steadied the sack as the other two hauled it up with their boat-hooks.

" Here it is ! " Marsdie said, as, with a muffled clang of metal, the sack fell on the deck again.

" You'd better hide it right in the cabin on the *Pride of Lancashire* itself," Mrs. Hallam decided. " Yon chap won't find it so easy to get it out of there when we're all in the saloon, I reckon."

" Good idea ! Help me to squeeze as much water out of the sack as I can, and to stow it under my bunk," Marsdie said.

They were busily engaged in lifting the sack from the butty boat to the *Pride of Lancashire* when they heard the sound of running feet. Mrs. Hallam's hand gripped the barge pole and her lips tightened in a straight line, but the runners proved only to be Roger with the rest of the party.

" I say, what's going on here ? Is anyone hurt ? " Roger shouted breathlessly.

" Oh, thank goodness Roger and Simon have come back ! " Ruth exclaimed.

" We heard shouts and Jonathan barking, so we ran all the way as fast as we could. What's the matter, Marsdie ? "

" A thief aboard the butty boat, but he got away. He was after the sack you found this morning, but he didn't get it. Jonathan flew at him and he dropped the sack in the canal," Marsdie explained. " We've just fished it out again and hidden it under my bunk."

" Good work, Marsdie ! " Roger warmly commended her.

Mrs. Hallam found she was trembling a little. " Oh, Roger, Miss Marsden had almost a stand-up fight with the thief. He struck her."

Roger turned quickly, in great concern, to Marsdie. " Oh, Marsdie, are you hurt ? "

" The blow glanced off my shoulder, luckily, Roger. But that man threatened to come back with others," Marsdie told him, a little troubled and fearful. The experience through which they had just passed was terrifying enough, without the threat of more to come.

" Then we'd better get the police at once," Roger decided promptly. " There's something queer about that sack, if the man tried to sneak it away like that. If it had been his property, why didn't he come and ask for it openly ? "

" I don't think you and I ought to leave the boat, Roger," Simon said dubiously. " That man's pretty certain to come back with others like himself."

" Which way did he go, Miss Marsden ? "
Sam interrupted.

" East, Sam, towards Appley Bridge.
Why ? " Miss Marsden asked.

" Listen, Roger. Dan and I can go the
opposite way, then, to Parbold, to get the
police. We can go on our cycles. We'll get
there in no time and bring help."

" Stout man, Sam ! Pass the cycles out to
them, Simon. Go as fast as you can. We
might have to deal with some very awkward
customers," Roger said.

" Do take care this time, Dan," Marsdie
warned Dan a little anxiously.

" Oh, I will, Marsdie. I promise. I'll make
up for this morning."

Dan and Sam mounted their bicycles and
were soon out of sight in the fast-gathering
shadows of the night.

" The thing to do is to gain time until
the police reach us," Simon declared. " I
think I know how we can do it. That sack,
Marsdie—can you empty the things out of it
quickly ? "

" Yes, Simon."

Marsdie ran into the cabin and tipped the
contents quickly under her bunk, then ran out
again with the sack.

" Good ! Now we'll fill it with stones and
sink it by the stern of the butty boat again.

It's that sack those men want, and I think they will look for it in the canal first, if we don't interfere with them.''

'' Good idea ! '' Roger applauded. '' Help to collect the stones, everyone.''

They scrambled about on the tow-path and in the nearby field, and soon the sack was partly filled with stones. As quickly and quietly as they could, Roger and Simon slung it overboard again by the stern of the butty boat at the place where Marsdie indicated.

'' They might go away with the sack full of stones, never knowing they'd been tricked,'' Ruth said hopefully.

'' Even if they don't, they'll waste time bringing it up out of the canal, and every minute will bring the police nearer to help us,'' Marsdie added.

'' Now we'd better go back into the cabin and just wait,'' Roger said.

It was shivery work waiting there, and even Mrs. Hallam looked a little paler than usual, and kept her hand ready on the barge pole, while Roger and Simon armed themselves with the boat-hooks, and, for want of a better weapon, Marsdie took up a large spanner.

'' If we have to put up a defence, we want to take them by surprise,'' Roger said. '' Marsdie, if the men come, dare you and

I   129

Mrs. Hallam pretend to tackle them alone at first, and then Simon and I will rush out at them ? They won't be expecting us."

" Yes," Mrs. Hallam said, stiffening her lips in a straight line. Marsdie nodded too, her face rather grim and set.

They had not long to wait, though even the few minutes in which they sat silent seemed an eternity. Then they heard running, stumbling feet approaching along the tow-path from the direction of Appley Bridge.

" Now ! " whispered Roger, and Marsdie grasped the spanner tighter yet.

" Huh ! Those two women have either disappeared or run away." Marsdie recognized the voice of their first unwelcome visitor. " So much the better for them," he went on. " The sack fell off the stern of that butty boat. Give me the boat-hook. We'll soon have it up."

He prodded and splashed about in the water astern of the butty boat, while the two other men shone electric torches over the water. At last he hooked it with the boat-hook and gave a powerful heave.

" Here it is ! " one of the men shouted. " Drop it on the tow-path, Bob."

The man addressed as Bob dropped the sack on the path, but instead of the clang of metal came the sharp tell-tale crash of stones. A second man was about to pick it up when he was stopped by the first one.

" Hi ! Wait a minute. That sounds queer to me. It doesn't sound like metal. Let's take a look inside."

The listeners in the cabin held their breath fearfully. The contents of the sack were tipped on the tow-path.

" Blimey ! Nothing but stones ! " the man called Bob exclaimed. " Someone has done the dirty on us. It's those two women in the boat. We'll soon show 'em ! " He stepped towards the *Pride of Lancashire*. " Hi, there!" he shouted.

" Get ready to do your stuff now, Marsdie," Roger whispered tensely.

Together Miss Marsden and Mrs. Hallam came up from the cabin. Miss Marsden was pale, but quite calm and collected.

" Well, what do you want ? " she addressed the men sharply.

" Hand over what was in this sack or it'll be the worse for you," the man blustered. " It belongs to us."

" No," Miss Marsden said firmly. " I do nothing for threats. Besides, what proof have I that it is your property ? "

" You'll know fast enough if we come aboard," the second man shouted at her. " Are you going to hand over that stuff ? "

" No ! " Miss Marsden defied him.

The first man moved in threatening fashion towards the boat. " Come on, Alf," he said to one of the other two men with him, " what are we waiting for ? There's nothing but a parcel of women and children aboard. I've watched them. I know."

" Put one foot on this boat and I'll set the dog on you again," Miss Marsden warned him.

" Get that sack ready to throw over the dog's head, Bob. A knife'll soon settle him," the second man said savagely.

" Aye, come on," Bob urged them.

Mrs. Hallam advanced and stood firmly by Miss Marsden. From where they stood they covered the exit from the cabin.

" You dare to come aboard and I'll knock you into the canal with this barge pole," Mrs. Hallam promised them fiercely.

" Come on ! " shouted the man known as Alf. " We're not going to be kept off that boat by a couple of women."

" Get back at once ! " Marsdie cried, advancing boldly with the spanner tightly gripped in her right hand.

" I'll let you have it if you come near me," Mrs. Hallam shouted, holding the barge pole as a knight of old might have held a tilting lance.

" Come on, Bob Todd ! " Alf said.

Bob Todd, together with Alf, leaped aboard the *Pride of Lancashire.*

" Come on, Simon," Roger whispered. " Here's where we take them by surprise. Ready ! "

Followed by Simon, he rushed up the ladder and on deck. Already Bob Todd had seized Miss Marsden by the arm.

" Take that ! " Roger cried, getting in a shrewd blow with the boat-hook. " And that ! "

With an oath the man let go his hold of Miss Marsden and turned to face a furious Roger. Before Alf could come to his assistance Simon had tackled him.

" And you take that ! " Simon said, dealing him a blow on his shins that brought him to his knees, though in a trice he was up again.

" Confound it ! There's more of them than we thought ! " he cried.

" They're nothing but a couple of lads," the third man cried, as he followed his mates on to the boat. " Come on, I tell you."

" They're armed with boat-hooks," Alf hesitated.

" So are we. Come on," Bob Todd said, making an ugly rush at Roger. But he reckoned without Mrs. Hallam.

Using the barge pole like a flail, Mrs. Hallam dashed to save Roger. Before her onslaught Bob Todd stepped back, but too late. The whirling barge pole caught him full on the chest, and over he toppled backwards into the canal with a mighty splash.

At that very moment, from the direction of Parbold, there came the sound of running feet.

" Hallo ! What's going on here ? " came in Cap'n Bill's voice. " Come on, Inspector Bannister. Come on."

" Now then, what are you up to, there ? " spoke the voice of authority. Then, as the other two men tried to elude Roger and slip away, the police officer shouted, " Come on, men, don't let them get away. Take them in the rear."

The light from Alf's torch fell for a moment on a uniformed figure.

" Crikey ! The police ! " he yelled. " Make a break for it, Joe."

Alf and Joe leaped ashore and dashed away along the two-path just as Inspector Bannister reached the boat.

" Oh, thank goodness ! It's Dan and Sam with Cap'n Bill and three policemen," Ruth gasped.

" Too late, lads. You've let them get away," the Inspector cried in disgust.

" No, not all of them. Look there ! There's one in the water," Mrs. Hallam shouted.

From the canal came a despairing cry. " Help ! Help ! I'm done for ! "

" Give me that boat-hook," Bannister said, snatching it from Simon's hands. " I'll fish him out. Grab hold of this, you rascal."

Bob Todd clutched wildly at it and held on desperately while Inspector Bannister drew him to the side and two stalwart policemen heaved him out.

" Oh ! Oh ! I'm finished ! " Todd gasped.

" Not you ! " Bannister said gruffly, turning him over and administering a rough first aid to pump the water out of his lungs. " Here ! Let's have a look at you."

He scrutinized the man's face with the aid of his torch, then he turned to Cap'n Fletcher.

" You were right, Cap'n Bill. This is Bob Todd right enough. He's the fellow we've been hunting for a long time."

Bob Todd sat up, brought round by this announcement almost quicker than by the Inspector's first aid.

" You've nothing on me, I tell you, you've nothing against me," he snivelled.

" Oh, haven't we ? What were you after on this boat when you attacked these ladies ? "

Bob Todd glared sullenly. He had no real

answer to this question. " You could hardly call it an attack," he muttered. " It was nothing but a bit of a push I gave the woman."

" Oh, you wicked fellow ! You struck Miss Marsden. You know you did ! " Mrs. Hallam exclaimed indignantly, and looked almost prepared to use the barge pole again.

" If we hadn't come along when we did, there's no knowing what might have happened, and you might have had to face a very serious charge," the Inspector told Todd grimly. " Now, what were you after ? "

Todd refused to reply.

" Wait a moment. I can show you what those men wanted," Miss Marsden said, and dashed into the cabin, followed by Roger. They returned in a few moments carrying the contents of the sack, piece by piece, which they placed on the deck at the Inspector's feet.

" All these things were in that sack," Marsdie said, pointing to the soaking sack which still lay on the tow-path. " The sack was in the cabin of the butty boat, and this man tried to take it first of all from there. It was the same sack that the boys took out of the canal at Adlington this morning."

The Inspector knelt on deck beside the exhibits and turned them over.

" Ah ! A stamping press. A metal lathe.

Some bars of nickel silver," he announced. " Very interesting indeed. I shall need these as evidence when I bring my case, so I'll take possession of them now, if you please, ma'am."

" If those lads found the sack in the canal at Adlington, then you can't pin anything on me," Bob Todd sneered. " You've nothing to prove that I dropped it in the canal."

Inspector Bannister glared at him for a moment and then said very sharply, " Turn out that man's pockets, Constable Smith."

The constable did so very promptly, and from a number of pockets came some thirty or forty new half-crowns. Todd's face fell as these came to light.

" Fond of new half-crowns, aren't you ? " Inspector Bannister asked him with some sarcasm. " We must show these to some of our experts on coinage, and see what they have to say about them, *and* these tools which came out of the sack. I think you're going to have quite a bit of explaining to do, Todd."

Todd had no answer and could only glare helplessly at the Inspector.

" You can take this chap to the police station, Constable Smith. See he gets some dry clothes," the Inspector gave his commands.

"Come down into the cabin, Inspector," Captain Fletcher invited him.

"Not just now, if you don't mind," the Inspector said. "I'll see Todd at the police station and get those other two rogues rounded up. They can't be far away, but I must do some telephoning and have them found. When that's done, I'll come back again, Cap'n Bill."

"Right. We'll be expecting you. Goodbye just now," the Captain replied. "Polly'll keep you something hot for supper."

For once Mrs. Hallam looked at a loss. "Eh, did you ever!" she exclaimed. "Do you know, Miss Marsden, we've forgotten all about supper. Well, I never knew that to happen before!"

Despite Mrs. Hallam's consternation at finding she had forgotten the supper, she managed to produce some very excellent macaroni and cheese by the time that Inspector Bannister returned to the *Pride of Lancashire* late that evening. Captain Fletcher steadfastly refused to enlighten them as to how he happened to come along just at the critical moment with Inspector Bannister and two policemen.

"Oh, we were on our way," he announced cryptically. "But I'll tell you the whole story when Inspector Bannister comes back, and he can fill in the details for me."

So Mrs. Hallam and the Brydons were forced to await the Inspector's return with impatience, while Cap'n Bill puffed away at his pipe with an enigmatical and satisfied smile on his face.

At last a light shone along the tow-path, and Inspector Bannister stepped aboard and was hailed warmly by the Captain and led to a seat at the table. Once the plates were all filled and the meal was well under way, Miss Marsden could restrain her curiosity no longer.

" You don't know how very glad we were to see you and Cap'n Bill this evening, Inspector," she began.

" Aye. We were coming along when we met Dan and Sam cycling along the tow-path in such a hurry that they almost ran into us, eh, lads ? " the Inspector laughed jovially. " But when we heard what they had to tell us, I reckon we were in a hurry too, and did a better bit of sprinting than we've done for years."

" We did, indeed," the Captain agreed. " Though I'd no notion that this was likely to happen when I asked you to join us aboard the *Pride of Lancashire* this evening."

" But what I can't understand is how you

came to have two constables with you as well. Had you asked them for supper, too, Cap'n Bill?" Ruth asked, far too innocently.

The Captain looked nonplussed for a moment, then he laughed. "Aye, you were too sharp for me there, Ruth. Well, I'd better confess that we were going a bit farther along the canal than the *Pride of Lancashire*. We meant to visit the *Crocus* first."

"But how did you know that the *Crocus* was just upstream from us, Cap'n Bill?" Simon asked this time. "They were still lying at Adlington when you left."

The Captain's eyes twinkled. "That's a good question too, Simon, but the truth is we had done a bit of telephoning to find out just where the *Crocus* was lying."

"That's correct," the Inspector corroborated. "They were able to tell us at Wigan Wharf that the *Crocus* had passed there, and then we tried the lock-keeper's cottage at Dean Lock, and we knew from his information that the barge couldn't be lying so far from the *Pride of Lancashire's* moorings."

The Brydons still looked mystified, and Captain Fletcher took up the story again to enlighten them.

"You see, it happened this way. After I'd paid that visit to the *Crocus* while you were climbing Rivington Pike, I felt very annoyed, for that fellow on the boat had treated me as no other canal folk would do. We're always interested in each other, you know, a kindly sort of interest, and there's not a single boatman but enjoys a chat with another in passing. It's our life, you see."

Inspector Bannister nodded. " That's right. Canal folk are proper friendly."

" So I began to think this chap on the *Crocus* wasn't a real canal boatman after all. At the same time I *knew* I'd seen his face somewhere before, but I couldn't think where for the life of me. I smoked my pipe and I thought and thought, and then I remembered I'd once seen his photograph in a newspaper when he'd been in the hands of the police before. Then, like a flash, it came to me that I'd heard he was wanted by the police in Liverpool again, and that he was Bob Todd."

" That was when you decided to go to Liverpool in a hurry ? " Susan asked.

" And you didn't tell us a word why you were going," Mrs. Hallam put in.

" That's right, Polly. You see, I didn't want to alarm you. I'd decided I'd look up my old friend Inspector Bannister and tell him what I'd found out. Now, you tell them the rest, Inspector."

The Inspector continued : " You see, there had been a lot of false half-crowns passed in and around shops and public houses in Liverpool, so it was plain that someone was coining them. We suspected Bob Todd might have something to do with it, for he'd been at the same game before. He's a good mechanic gone wrong. He'd disappeared from his usual haunts and we couldn't locate his hide-out, nor where his workshop was, if he were making the half-crowns."

The Inspector paused, and Cap'n Bill went on with the story once more. " And then I told the Inspector about the *Crocus* and how her engines were being run even when she was moored, and how there didn't really appear to be any engine trouble, either."

" It came to me like a flash that the half-crowns were being coined aboard that boat," Inspector Bannister continued. " They could use their Diesel engine for the job without rousing much suspicion. All they needed to do was to moor in a quiet place, and pretend to all and sundry that they'd got a bit of engine trouble. But they didn't count on the generous helpful nature of Cap'n Bill where engine trouble was concerned," Inspector Bannister chuckled. " Aye, you got them worried there, Bill, all right."

" But why did they tip part of their tools in

the canal at Adlington ? " Roger wanted to know.

" Because Captain Bill was a bit too nosey about their engines and their cargo. They feared he was suspicious of them, or even that he'd been set on to question them by the police. Guilty men are always fearful. They were afraid of a visit from the police next, so they placed the incriminating tools in a sack in case the barge was searched, and then they sank the sack in a marked spot—opposite a certain tree you said you found it—where they could easily fish it out again when all was quiet."

" And then Dan rode his cycle into the water and upset all their plans," Simon said.

" Exactly ! They must have posted someone in that little woodland at the ege of the water to keep an eye on the sack. That man saw what happened and how, in searching for the bicycle, you fished the sack out of the canal too. He quickly got in touch with the others who were aboard the *Crocus*, and after that they trailed you on your cruise as closely as they dared."

" And they tried to have a look for the sack aboard the *Pride of Lancashire* at Wigan Wharf," Miss Marsden put in.

The Inspector nodded. " Yes, but the

wharfman and your dog were too much for
them, so they just followed you up to a quiet
place and watched for their opportunity. I
think when Bob Todd got the sack from the
butty boat he was under the impression you
were all ashore and had gone for a long walk,
Dog Jonathan as well."

" Only, as it happened, Miss Marsden and I
had stayed aboard to have forty winks, and
the *Pride of Lancashire* was all quiet and in
darkness," Mrs. Hallam explained.

" It's jolly lucky we wakened in time, and
were able to tackle him before he was off with
the sack," Marsdie said.

" Marsdie, you were absolutely splendid.
Oh, I wish you could all have seen how she
stood up to that awful man," Ruth told the
others.

Miss Marsden, however, disclaimed the
credit. " Oh, you've Mrs. Hallam to thank
that he dropped the sack in the water. She
was jolly handy with a barge pole."

Mrs. Hallam shook her head modestly too.
" I think Jonathan really saved the day," she
declared.

Dan patted his old friend. " Good dog,
Jonathan. Have another biscuit," he offered
generously, and no one forbade him. Jonathan
gave a joyous yelp of gratitude, and Dan
looked round the assembled company in pride.

" Well, aren't you jolly glad I brought him ? " he demanded.

" Oh, we are, Dan, we are ! " Marsdie admitted frankly, speaking for the rest of the family.

Captain Fletcher looked from one to the other of them rather anxiously as he filled his pipe.

" I suppose after all this you'll be anxious to get back to Milchester," he said. " You won't want any more canal cruising."

" Won't we ? Of course we will. You try us and see. We want to go all the way to Liverpool and back," came in a chorus from everyone.

Captain Fletcher looked pleased. " Liverpool it shall be then. And after that, back home the way we came to Cherry Tree Wharf ? "

" Rather ! Of course ! " everyone said.

Captain Fletcher beamed at them. " I've got a *grand* crew, Inspector Bannister," he said.

" We'll sail with you all the holidays if you like, Cap'n Bill," Dan offered.

Cap'n Bill hardly knew how to receive this staggering announcement, but Marsdie, with a twinkle in her eye, saved his embarrassment by saying, " But don't forget the Milchester Show, Dan. We shall all want to be home in good time to prepare for that, so at any rate, Cap'n Bill, you'll be saved from sailing on and on for ever with us, like the Flying Dutchman."

" If the Flying Dutchman had so good a crew for company, I reckon he wasn't so badly off," the Captain replied gallantly, with an answering twinkle in his eye.

Chapter Six

DAN AND SAM EXPERIMENT

NOT long after the Brydons' return from their canal trip, it was time for the Milchester Annual Show. This was the great event of the year in Milchester, for everyone in the village took part in it, and farm folk for many miles around made it the occasion for a jaunt and a meeting with friends. There were all kinds of exhibits, from small pigs to prize cabbages. There were competition classes for which everyone could enter, old or young : classes for cake-making, for preserves, for pickles, for hand-knitted garments, and for craft work, besides the usual classes for vegetables and flowers. There were special classes in which children could compete. On this occasion there were feverish preparations for the Show, not only in every Milchester home, but by the Brydons at One Elm Cottage, and at St. Jonathan's Hospital next door, where many of the small patients were entering exhibits in the Handicrafts sections. Simon and Roger together were entering their best vegetables and fruit, for, if Simon did the work of planting in the late spring when Roger was at the university in London, Roger still laboured in his " borrowed garden " at Beech-acres throughout his long summer vacation.

The week preceding the Show had been very wet indeed, with deluges of rain, and many were the anxious glances cast at the sky : barometers were incessantly tapped, and the B.B.C. weather forecasts became more important than the news to Milchester ears.

Miss Marsden emptied the contents of a huge parcel on to the kitchen table at One Elm Cottage, and looked over them with justifiable pride.

" Susan, will you help me to pack up all this embroidery, and these leather bags and purses, that the little people of St. Jonathan's have made ? They're entering them for the competitions at the Milchester Show."

" Certainly, Marsdie. Oh, what a lovely lot ! Aren't they pretty ? " Susan exclaimed with delight.

Miss Marsden looked pleased. " Yes, I think they are. Look at this nightdress-case shaped like a flower that Doris Dawson sewed."

" It's beautiful, and she never did any embroidery at all till you taught her, did she, Marsdie ? " Susan commented.

" No. This was one of her first attempts."

Ruth came from the scullery where she had been doing some baking. " May I look too ? Oh, see ! What a quaint little purse ! It's shaped just like a pansy face, and the leather is all tooled and stained to make it look like a pansy."

" Yes, Tommy Robinson made that one," Marsdie told them. It is rather original, isn't it ? Really, I wish I could give every one of them a prize, they have all tried so hard."

" I think you should have a prize for teaching them so well, Marsdie," Ruth said.

Miss Marsden spent the greater part of her day at Beechacres teaching the little crippled patients there how to use their hands in making beautiful articles of leather embroidery and raffia-work.

" Spare my blushes, Ruth," she said modestly. " Is your cake made yet ? "

" Yes, but not iced. Mrs. Hallam and I are both having a private competition to see who can beat the other. Mr. Cameron has promised to be the judge."

There was a step at the door and in came Mr. Cameron. He had just caught the drift of Ruth's last remark, and he grinned impishly.

" Yes, Ruth Brydon, but that's only on condition that I get a whacking big slice out of each cake, and I'm not sure that my decision won't depend on the size of the slice ! " he informed them.

" Oh, hallo, Mr. Cameron ! I never heard you come in," Miss Marsden exclaimed.

" You were so terribly busy with all those entrancing little articles. Dr. Brydon sent me across to say that she had to go to Preston to order some very necessary medical supplies, and she wanted to know if there was anything she could bring back for you."

" Some tissue paper in pretty colours would be a help in displaying these handicraft entries," Miss Marsden said. " Just a small quantity would be sufficient."

" Right ! I'll tell her. She's going by the morning train, and returning by the one in the late afternoon that leaves Preston just after five o'clock. Will that do ? "

" Oh, splendidly," Miss Marsden replied. " It will give us the whole evening to mount the exhibits."

" Please ask Mother to bring some drawing-pins back with her too, Mr. Cameron," Susan asked. " They're always sold out at Milchester Post Office."

" Very well, Susan, I'll remember. Let's hope this rain doesn't spoil your exhibits, Roger," Mr. Cameron remarked.

" I hope not," Roger replied, casting a rather

gloomy glance through the kitchen window at the leaden skies. "The rain's still pelting down. If it keeps on like this till Saturday it will completely ruin the show."

"Surely it will clear before then," Marsdie said hopefully. "I'm afraid the field will be pretty wet as it is. If only a good stiff wind would spring up——"

"Do you know, Mr. Cameron, Marsdie is the only one of us who hasn't got an exhibit in the Show," Susan told him. "Ruth's entering a cake. I've made something for the knitting competition. Roger and Simon are exhibiting vegetables, and Dan and Sam ought to win a prize with their rabbits. There's only Marsdie left out of it."

"Shame! Shame, Miss Marsden," Mr. Cameron teased her.

"It's because she's been helping everyone else, that's why," Ruth protested. "Marsdie's had no time to do anything herself."

"But what could I do?" Marsdie asked. "If I made a cake I'd be hopelessly outclassed by Ruth and Mrs. Hallam, even if I remembered to put in half the ingredients. I haven't time to knit, and I know Susan beats me at that. Now, if only there was a class for *pickles*, I might have entered. I really am clever at making pickles. I used to love pickling beetroot . . ."

" But, Marsdie, there *is* a class for pickles,"
Roger interrupted.

" Now stop leading me up the garden path,
Roger."

" But there is, truly," Roger insisted.
" Here's the list of competitors' classes in my
pocket. See ! ' Pickles : A jar of any kind
of pickle or chutney. More than one exhibit
may be offered by a competitor '. There ! "

" Well, if only I'd known . . ." Marsdie
was beginning, but Roger was not going to let
her slide out of it so easily.

" It's not too late yet, Marsdie. There are
the vegetables to hand in the garden. I'll
bring you what you want ! "

" Go on, Marsdie. You've got nearly a whole
day to make them in," Ruth urged her.

" Yes, go on, Marsdie. Produce these
perfectly phenomenal pickles you so proudly
brag about," Roger declared.

" Oh, don't, Roger ! " Marsdie laughed.
" Your tongue will be tied in knots. Besides, I
need some other ingredients besides vegetables."

" What ? " Roger asked.

" Well, I'll require an ounce of purmeric
and some tickling spice," Marsdie said quite
seriously, entirely unprepared for the burst of
laughter that followed her remark.

" *Tickling* spice, Marsdie ? What's that ? "
Roger grinned.

" Oh dear, Roger ! Now you've got me all tongue-tied. I mean an ounce of turmeric and some pickling spice," Marsdie explained.

" What's turmeric ? " Susan asked. " Some witch's sinister brew, Marsdie ? "

" No, Susan, it's simply a vegetable dye to make mustard pickle look more yellow. That reminds me—I'll need mustard too, and simply quarts of vinegar."

" Good gracious ! Is Marsdie contemplating a pickle factory now ? " Roger exclaimed.

" Oh, I may as well do the thing properly," Marsdie said. " I'm going to enter two kinds of pickle—piccalilli and spiced beetroot. Now you've got me worked up, nothing shall stop me. I've become pickle-minded——"

A roar of laughter interrupted her.

" Now what have I said ? " she wanted to know. " Anyway, I can always sell what's over to make funds for St. Jonathan's."

" That's right, Marsdie," Mr. Cameron applauded. " We shall want to have a Christmas party again, and funds are getting low."

The door opened suddenly and in came Simon.

" Hallo, everyone ! " he said, his face beaming. " I say, Marsdie, wonderful news ! Mr. Benton says the committee of the Milchester Show are going to ask competitors to let their entries be sold at the end of the Show and the money is to be given to St. Jonathan's funds."

" Oh, Simon, how wonderful ! " Marsdie cried.

" But Mr. Benton wants us all to help with the selling afterwards," Simon added.

" Willingly ! " everyone cried.

" They're going to put up a big stall at the end of the marquee to which people can take their gifts, and Mr. Benton asks if you'll come to the marquee this afternoon and decorate it. There's lots of bunting you can have, he says."

" Isn't that splendid ? " Ruth exclaimed. " We'll all come along and help too, Marsdie."

" It's just like the kind folk of Milchester," Marsdie beamed. " But goodness, what a busy day I'm going to have ! These handicraft entries——"

" We'll help with them," Susan said at once.

" And the pickles. Really, I think I'll have to relinquish the idea of the pickles——" Marsdie was beginning when she was silenced by a storm of protest.

" Oh, no, Marsdie, no ! You mustn't ! "

" Then I'll have to get the ingredients quickly. I must go to the village this morning and get them."

" Couldn't Dan and Sam go to Fawcett's shop for them ? " Simon suggested, but Ruth poured scorn on this idea.

" You know what it's like when Dan and Sam go shopping. It takes *hours*, and they have to have a chat with everyone in Milchester."

" I'll go, Marsdie," Susan volunteered.

" Thank you, Susan," Marsdie said gratefully.

" By the way, where are Dan and Sam ? " Mr. Cameron inquired. " I haven't seen them about to-day."

Simon laughed. " Oh, since Sam Mitton got hold of a book *Chemistry for the Young Beginner*, they've become chemistry-conscious."

" Yes, they've begged Marsdie to let them work in the scullery and use the gas-stove for their experiments. That's where they are now."

" Oh, Marsdie, how foolish," Roger declared with a chuckle.

Marsdie looked a little uncertain. " Well, they did beg so hard, and they both shared the top place in science at school this term," she explained. " They really deserve some encouragement."

" It'll be all right if you don't go and mistake some of their concoctions for the soup at

dinner-time, Marsdie, and poison us all,"
Roger declared.

" Oh, Roger, what a frightful thought ! "
Marsdie exclaimed, quite appalled.

" It's very interesting all the same. What
are they doing now ? " Mr. Cameron asked.

Hardly were the words out of his mouth
when there came the most appalling report
from the scullery, accompanied by the crash
of shattering glass.

" Oh, whatever's happened ? " Marsdie
exclaimed, turning quite pale.

" They've blown themselves up ! " Simon
cried in the same breath.

" Oh, Dan ! Sam ! Are you all right ? "
Ruth shouted.

" Is anyone hurt ? " Mr. Cameron said as he
started for the scullery door, but Roger got
there before him.

" What's happened in here ? " he cried, as
he flung the door open. " Are you hurt, either
of you ? "

Through the fumes he perceived Dan and
Sam staring in a stricken fashion at the debris.
Glass littered the table and floor everywhere.

" Goodness ! What a sight ! " Roger said.

Marsdie dashed to Dan, who was still looking a little dazed.

" Oh, Dan, your hand's bleeding," she said
in consternation.

" What's happened in here ? "

" It's all right, Marsdie, really it is," Dan protested. " It's only a very little scratch."

" Come to the window and let me have a look at it," Marsdie insisted. " Mercy me ! You've even got glass in your hair."

" Are you all right, Sam ? " Ruth asked.

" Quite all right, Ruth, thank you." Sam surveyed the litter with a crestfallen air. " Eh, Miss Marsden, I'm proper sorry about all this mess."

" There's glass everywhere, even sticking in the curtains," Simon pointed out.

" What were you doing, you priceless little idiots ? " Roger asked rather crossly. He knew that Marsdie had had a nasty shock.

" We were trying to make hydrogen," Sam explained.

" Make hydrogen ! " Simon cried. " Why, you've no business to be doing that outside the school laboratories."

" Something must have gone wrong with the apparatus," Sam said, stating the obvious.

" There's something badly wrong with it now," Roger said grimly, surveying the mess. " What had you done ? "

" It was my fault. Sam did say he thought the end of the thistle funnel should be under the water," Dan admitted.

" You see, the gas wasn't coming out of the little glass tube at the side, so Dan struck a match and tried to see if it would light at the thistle funnel instead," Sam went on to explain further.

" It was then everything happened," Dan said mournfully.

" My goodness ! No wonder it did ! Dan, you are a little donkey," Simon said candidly.

Now that the first fright was over, annoyance with the culprits began to take its place.

" Just look at all the mess you've made, on such a busy day, too," Ruth scolded.

" Well, let's be thankful it's no worse," Marsdie tried to smooth everyone down. " It's a good thing neither of them lost their eyesight. A bit of sticking-plaster is all that Dan's scratch needs, thank goodness."

" Where did you get your apparatus ? " Mr. Cameron asked, feeling a little sorry for the two boys.

" Mr. Armstrong from the new factory lent it to us, so that we could experiment," Sam said ruefully.

" Well, a nice mess it's in now," Simon declared.

" I'd no idea you were going to try any dangerous experiments, Dan, or I would never have given you permission to use the gas-stove," even Marsdie said rather severely.

Dan looked contrite. " I'm sorry, Marsdie. I didn't know it would go off like that."

" You can jolly well clear it all up and sweep the glass from everywhere and put it in the dustbin and scrub down the table afterwards," Ruth told them.

" All right. We will, Ruth, only don't be so bossy," Dan said, recovering his spirits a little. " Every famous scientist has to experiment at first."

" Famous scientists my foot," Roger squashed him. " You always have to go and do something daft on the busiest days, Dan."

" We were top in chemistry anyway, Roger Brydon," Dan said haughtily. " Weren't we, Sam ? "

" Aye, Dan, but I reckon we've still got to learn a bit before we're finished," Sam said modestly. " Don't worry, Miss Marsden, we'll clear up the mess all right and leave everything tidy."

" All right, Sam. I'm only thankful that neither of you was seriously hurt," Miss Marsden said kindly.

" Just look at the time," Roger said, glancing at the clock. " Simon and I have promised to give a hand with the setting up of the marquee and the stalls inside it. Come along, Simon."

" Yes, but there are the vegetables to get for Marsdie's pickles first," Simon reminded him.

" Oh, yes, we mustn't forget those. It won't

take us more than a few minutes." Roger went to the door and poked his head outside. " Oh, look, the rain's off ! Thank goodness ! If only we can get the marquee and tents up while it is still dry——"

" I'll skip down to Mrs. Fawcett's and get the pickling spice and the turmeric stuff," Susan said.

" There are still a lot of the children's exhibits over at St. Jonathan's. Will you come across with me, Ruth, and help me to sort them out ? And afterwards we must go and decorate that stall when we think the marquee will be up," Marsdie asked.

" With pleasure, Marsdie."

" I'll be getting back to St. Jonathan's too before Dr. Brydon starts off for Preston," Mr. Cameron said.

When the door had closed behind everybody, Dan looked mournfully at the debris of their unfortunate experiment, and sighed, " They've all gone out now but us."

Sam Mitton was more inclined to take a philosophic view of it. " Come on, Dan. It could have been a lot worse. Get a brush and sweep this up, lad, while I fetch a bucket and a mop."

" You know, Sam, I don't think anybody really *appreciates* us and our work," Dan remarked in an injured tone.

" Well, you could hardly expect them all to go into raptures over this 'ere, could you ? " Sam replied practically.

" But they might think what all this is leading up to, Sam," Dan said with dignity. " Don't they realize that we're working for— for *humanity* ? "

" Are we ? " Sam asked, in some surprise.

" Of course we are ! Aren't we going to find something that'll put an end to atomic bombs ? " Dan answered grandly.

Sam scratched his head and looked at the litter everywhere about them. " Well, we seem to have gone a rum way about doing it," he remarked. " Jolly nearly blew up One Elm Cottage, we did ! "

" Oh, that was just an accident," Dan said airily. " We shall do better next time."

" From the look in Miss Marsden's eye, I don't think there'll be a next time," Sam said mournfully.

" We've got to begin at the beginning and learn as we go on, of course," Dan admitted.

" Aye, it seems there's a good chance of us going on—through the roof ! " Sam replied with some sarcasm. " What about that brush and mop, Dan ? "

" Bother the brush ! " Dan said. " You know, Sam, it hurts when people don't appreciate you. Roger said we were priceless idiots."

Dan's sense of injury began to grow hot within him.

" 'Appen Roger was a bit put out, like," Sam agreed.

" And Ruth was very horrid about the mess, too," Dan went on. " Maybe some day, when we're great scientists, they'll be sorry about this."

" 'Appen ! " Sam said laconically, as one who had grave doubts on the matter, wielding the brush with energy while Dan stood on his dignity and held forth.

" It's just because we're always around that they don't value us," Dan continued. " I tell you, Sam, Roger'll be wanting someone to fetch and carry all those vegetables for him to the marquee this afternoon."

" Yes ? " Sam said, not paying any very serious attention, being more engaged with the task of cleaning up the litter.

" Well, we're not going to be here, that's all," Dan announced with grim decision. This did make Sam stop in his task and take notice.

" Why ? " he asked.

" People begin to miss you when you're not so handy and obliging," Dan said. " We'll go fishing instead, where the Black Brook runs into the river."

Sam paused with the brush in his hand and stared at Dan. " But the river'll be in spate after all this rain. There won't be any fish rising."

" There may be," Dan retorted obstinately. " You don't know, Sam. We'll go and see."

" Oh, all right," Sam agreed, seeing that Dan was so set on it. " But we've got to clear up this mess."

Dan saw the sense of this, and set to work at last with a will.

As soon as dinner was over the two boys rushed off with Dan's fishing-rod in their hands, and when Susan came through the green door from Beechacres she encountered them. Both stopped short with a guilty air, and Susan opened her eyes wide in amazement.

" Hallo, where are you going with that fishing rod ? " she asked.

" Oh, bother ! " Dan said under his breath. Aloud he replied airily, " Oh, we're just off to do a bit of fishing, that's all."

" What ? In all this rain ? " Susan asked.

" It isn't raining just now," Dan told her.

Susan glanced up at the leaden lowering skies. " Well, not at the moment," she agreed, " but it's jolly well going to. Just look at all those *terrific* clouds ! I've never seen the sky so dark."

" It'll probably blow over." Dan gave way to a little wishful thinking.

" You'd better not go far if you don't want to be drenched," Susan warned them.

" We're just going as far as the Black Brook, Susan," Sam informed her.

" Goodness ! That's far enough," Susan exclaimed. " You'll be wanted to help with the things for the Show too, remember."

" Oh, we'll be back in heaps of time for that," Dan said carelessly. Then he stopped short. " Look here, Susan, do be a sport and promise not to tell Roger and Simon where we've gone."

Susan was rather surprised at this request. " Why not ? " she asked.

Dan looked rather aggrieved. " I'm rather vexed with Roger. It was very horrid of him to call us priceless idiots when that flask exploded this morning. *Anyone* can have an accident."

Susan laughed. Apparently this was one of Dan's moments when he was on his dignity. Susan knew quite well that before very long Dan would have forgotten about it altogether. He was feeling sore about it at the time, but Dan never bore anyone a grudge for very long.

" All right. I won't tell," she promised. " But don't be away long, and if it starts to rain you'd better come straight home."

" Oh, all right. Don't fuss," Dan said. " Come along, Sam."

Together they hurried away down the road.

They could hardly have reached the Black Brook when Simon came dashing into One Elm Cottage.

" I say, Susan, have you seen Dan and Sam anywhere about ? " he cried.

Susan was just about to tell Simon where the two truants were when she remembered her promise to Dan.

" Er—yes—I did see them earlier in the afternoon. Why, Simon ? "

" Mr. Benton asked me to remind them that they have to provide rabbit-hutches for the rabbits they are showing. They must have their hutches in position in the marquee not later than six o'clock this evening."

" Oh, is the marquee up ? " Susan asked.

" Yes, thank goodness we got it up while the rain held off, for it's going to pour soon."

" Why have they to be there so early with their hutches ? " Susan asked, throwing a glance at the clock. " The Show isn't till to-morrow afternoon."

" You couldn't have people staggering in with dozens of rabbit hutches in all the crowds that will be there to-morrow, sticking them down anywhere in the marquee, could you now ? " Simon asked.

Susan saw the sense of this. " I suppose not, Simon."

" That's why the committee made the rule that the rabbit-hutches must be placed in position to-day, otherwise the entries will be disqualified."

" Oh dear ! I don't think Dan and Sam knew about that," Susan said.

" Of course, the rabbits don't have to be taken there till to-morrow, but I thought Dan didn't know about the hutches, and I didn't want him to be disqualified. He has some good rabbits this year. Time's getting on. Where have they gone ? "

Susan hesitated. " I—I'm not quite sure where they are just at this minute, Simon, but I think I know where to look for them. Leave it to me."

" All right," Simon said. " But don't leave it too late. It will soon be tea-time. And if you go hunting for them be sure to put on your rainproof. It's going to rain jolly hard. There are one or two spots already."

Susan gave a glance outside. " Gracious me, yes ! I'll take Dan's mackintosh with me too, and that old oilskin cape for Sam."

" Right, then, Susan, I'll leave it to you. I've got to go back to the marquee. Tell Marsdie not to wait for Roger and me at tea-time. I'm not sure when we'll be back, or Ruth either."

" All right. Bye-bye, Simon," Susan said.

As soon as the door closed behind Simon,

she began to look for her rainproof and Dan's. Hers was hanging on its customary peg in the hall, but Dan's was nowhere to be seen.

" Where on earth has Dan put it ? " Susan exclaimed in exasperation ; then she spotted it at the bottom of the hall cupboard lying in a heap.

" Just like Dan ! " she said as she shook it. " Now for Marsdie's oilskin cape for Sam. Dear me ! It's beginning to rain hard. I must hurry ! " she cried, banging the door behind her and rushing along to the crossroads, where she would take the turning on to a side road leading down to the river and the Black Brook.

Chapter Seven

THE BRYDONS IN A PICKLE

WHEN Dan and Sam reached the Black Brook they were astonished to find the stream in full spate, a brown, rushing, boiling turmoil of waters little short of a raging torrent. Sam surveyed it with dismay.

" I'd no idea it would be like this. There'll be no fishing in this, Dan," Sam declared. " You'd just get your line torn clean off your rod."

" Perhaps it will be better down at the river," said Dan, the ever-hopeful one.

They left the Black Brook and scrambled down the rocky lane towards the river. As they went the sky became more and more darkly threatening.

" I say, it is getting darker ! " Sam said with apprehension. A distant rumble punctuated his words. " Listen ! That's thunder ! " he exclaimed.

When they reached the river they found the conditions there were, if anything, worse than they had been at the brook.

169

" Look ! How high the river is ! " Dan cried. " It's just rushing along under that little stone bridge by the old mill. If it gets much higher, it'll be as high as the bridge itself."

True, there was only a matter of a couple of feet between the arch of the bridge and the swollen waters.

" Aye, and the flood's seeping over the footpath at the side here now," Sam pointed out. " There'll be no fish in this flood, Dan. We're just wasting our time."

" It seems like it," Dan agreed gloomily. " I'd no idea the river was such a torrent as this."

" It's been raining heavily all week, you know," Sam reminded him. " Gosh ! Here comes the rain again. Watch it splash on the water. I wish we'd brought our raincoats."

" Perhaps it will only be a shower," Dan said. " Mercy me, though, just listen to that thunder. It's coming nearer."

There was a much louder roll of thunder.

" Here comes the rain," Sam shouted as the heavens seemed to open.

" Can we shelter under the bridge ? " Dan asked.

" Well, does it look like it, lad ? " Sam said with heavy sarcasm. " Not unless you want to be swept away with the flood. We'd better make for the old ruined mill."

" But there's no roof on it," Dan objected.

" Yes, there's one part where there's still a bit of roof left," Sam told him. " Come along. Run, or you'll be drenched."

Together they sprinted along the river path towards the old mill. As they went there was a vivid flash of lightning followed by a terrific crack of thunder. Even Dan looked startled. Sam ran harder still.

" Come on. It won't do to be caught in the open with all these big trees about," he shouted over his shoulder to Dan. " Run ! Here's the old mill door. Get inside quickly. Look, there's a corner over there where the roof hasn't fallen in. Get under it. Mind those old beams."

Dan, recovering his breath, said miserably, quite forgetting that he had suggested the expedition, " I wish we hadn't come. I'm wet already. We might have to stay here for hours."

" Aye, it looks fair set in," Sam agreed. " All the same, we'd better wait here a bit. You'll get an awful row if you turn up at One Elm Cottage soaked to the skin, on the top of what happened this morning."

Dan saw the sense of this, and settled himself beside Sam on a big stone to wait for the weather to clear ; but the skies still became darker and darker, and the deluge did not abate.

As Susan ran as fast as she was able towards the Black Brook, the rain began to come down in earnest. Then, from the direction of Pendle Hill, invisible among the clouds, there came a distant roll of thunder. Susan always hated thunder and shivered a little.

" Oh dear ! Oh dear ! " she gasped as she ran, " there's the thunder ! I do feel frightened. What big drops of rain ! I hope I find Dan and Sam before it gets too heavy."

She tried to quicken her steps, and her breath came in short sobbing gasps. As she reached the Black Brook she cried, " Da-an ! Sam ! Da-an ! " but there was no reply, neither were they to be seen anywhere. Thinking that perhaps Dan had chosen to go down to the river itself, she ran in that direction. When she reached the river she halted, frightened and appalled at the sight of this torrent of waters brimming over and lipping the banks. Another roll of thunder, much heavier this time, added to her panic.

" Da-an ! Sam ! " she shrieked, despairing that her voice could be heard above the roar of the waters.

In the shelter of the mill Dan was just saying

gloomily, " It's an awful storm, Sam, I wish we were home."

" So do I. I think we were daft to come here on a day like this," Sam retorted, for once rather crossly, when Susan's long-drawn-out call reached his ears faintly. " Listen ! What was that ? " he said, laying an urgent hand upon Dan's arm.

" What ? I didn't hear anything," Dan said.

" It sounded like someone calling. Listen ! "

They both sat perfectly still and silent, and then again there came the wail over the noise of the storm, " Da-an ! Sam ! "

" It's Susan ! " Dan cried.

" Let's run to the front of the mill and let her know where we are," Sam said, starting to run, and at the same time calling out, " Here we are, Susan. Over at the mill ! Susan ! "

In a moment he sighted Susan on the other side of the river, and Susan eyed the boiling torrent between them in despair.

" Oh dear ! You're on the other side of the river ! " she cried.

" It's all right. There's a little bridge just up yonder," Dan told her. " Come over it, Susan. There's some shelter in the mill."

" Oh, the river's right up to the arch of the bridge. I'm afraid to cross," she cried.

" Take a run at it, Susan," Sam encouraged her. " You'll be across it in a second."

Susan hesitated, then, summoning all her courage to help her, she took a deep breath and darted across the bridge, while the racing waters seethed and thundered below. Sam was waiting for her and seized her by the hand, running with her towards the shelter of the mill.

" Oh dear, Sam ! We'll never dare to go back that way if the river rises any higher," Susan declared, throwing a fearful glance over her shoulder. " Oh, what a downpour ! I thought I'd never find you. I was so frightened."

" We're sheltering in the old mill. There's a bit of a roof there," Sam gasped as they ran.

" Here's the place, Susan," Dan gasped thankfully. " At any rate, it will keep the rain off."

" Here are your raincoats," Susan said, ruefully regarding the already wet garments over her arm. " They look pretty wet."

" The insides are dry, anyway, and they'll help to keep us warm," Dan said gratefully, giving a slight shiver. " It was jolly good of you to come after us like that, Susan."

" I promised Simon I'd find you, you see," Susan explained. " He came back to say that you had to have your rabbit-hutch down at the marquee by six o'clock to-night or you wouldn't be allowed to show Peter the Giant, and there wasn't a lot of time."

" Thanks a lot, Susan," Dan said gratefully. " We'd better be getting back to Milchester."

" Not in this downpour, lad. Talk sense ! " Sam Mitton told Dan quite sharply for once.

Just then there was a most vivid flash of lightning, followed by the crash of thunder, this time very loud and near. Susan shuddered.

" We'd better stay here," she said. " We shouldn't be safe outside."

Scarcely had she spoken and the roll of the thunder died away than there was another terrific flash, with an instantaneous crack that was deafening. It was followed by the crash of falling masonry near at hand.

" Oh, whatever's that ? " Susan shrieked.

" Mercy me ! Has the mill been struck by lightning ? " Dan cried. Even he grew a little. pale.

" No, it wasn't quite as near as that," Sam said. " You wait here with Susan. I'm going out to see."

" Then I'm coming too," Dan declared.

" So am I," Susan said fearfully. " I don't want to be left here alone in this thunderstorm."

Holding hands they ran out from the ruins of the mill on to the river bank.

" Oh, the bridge ! " Sam cried.

" It's gone ! " Susan exclaimed, aghast.

There, with the waters racing and swirling about it, was the collapsed heap of stones which had been the bridge. Wedged against it like a huge battering-ram was the fallen trunk of a big tree, its branches entangled among the stones. Other debris coming down the river began to pile up against it.

" Oh, what shall we do ? " Susan cried, wringing her hands. " The bridge is just a heap of ruins. How are we to get back to Milchester now ? "

" It's all right, Susan. There's a wooden footbridge higher up the river. We can go back that way," Dan comforted her.

Sam said nothing. He was surveying the ruined bridge with something like consternation.

" But I say ! Look what's happening," he said. " The bridge has fallen right into the river, and with that tree wedged against it, it's making a kind of dam. Everything that's coming down the river, all those torn branches, are lodging against it and can't get past, and look how the water's piling up behind the barrier already and spreading out over the path."

"Goodness, yes! If that breaks, it might sweep the mill and everything away," Dan exclaimed, seeing the immediate danger.

"We'd better hurry to get higher up the river to the footbridge before the path is altogether under water," Susan cried.

Sam, however, was seeing beyond the actual immediate peril.

"Aye, we'd better be moving, but that's not the worst," he told them. "If the river overflows just here, it'll flood the railway line just beyond there, on the other side. Come along, get higher up the bank and then we can see better."

Scrambling upwards away from the already inundated path, the children gained the top of the bank and looked down on the scene below them. The bank on the other side was much lower, and fell away to a stretch of rather rough swampy meadow at a slightly lower level than the path itself. Already the river, prevented from taking its normal channel by the barrier of the fallen tree and bridge, was pouring over the path and into the meadow, taking a new course for itself, and that course led straight for the low railway embankment.

"The river's just pouring towards the line," Sam cried. "The embankment's not very high there either. If it gets swept away——"

Susan saw at once what Sam meant. "Come

" The river's washed away part of the embankment
already ! "

along. Let's run for the other footbridge,"
she said. " We must try to get to Milchester
as soon as we can and warn someone."

Luckily the wooden footbridge was standing
as firmly as ever.   As they raced across it they
had a better view of the river and what was
happening down below.   They slackened speed
a little in horror.

" Oh, look ! " Susan cried.   " The river's
washed away part of the railway embankment
already ! "

The soil and cinder track upon which the

embankment was built was being hollowed out by the force of the water, and, as they watched, a section of it collapsed like a sand-castle in the path of the tide, leaving the rail suspended above, without support beneath it.

" That rail would give way altogether if a train was to come over it," Sam cried. Then, in dismay, he clutched Dan by the arm. " Oh, Dan, the 5.3 out of Preston is due in Milchester in less than a quarter of an hour. It's got to pass over that stretch of line. We've got to do something to stop it. We *must* reach the signal-box."

" Oh, Dan ! " Susan exclaimed, her hand on her heart, " Mother will be on that train. I heard Mr. Cameron tell Marsdie she was coming back from Preston by it. Oh, we must stop it. We must ! We must ! Where's the nearest signal-box, Sam ? "

" A mile farther up the road," Sam said soberly.

" Oh, we'll never make it, never ! " Susan shrieked in a panic.

" We must ! Run ! Run ! " Dan urged the others, dragging Susan along with him.

" Wait ! " Sam commanded. " We'll never make it if we stick to the road, but we might just manage it if we went along the railway line and through yon tunnel. It 'ud only take five minutes through the tunnel."

Susan faltered a little. " The tunnel! Oh! It's pitch dark. Suppose we met a train in it, Sam ? "

" I've got a torch in my pocket. *I'll* run through the tunnel, Susan," Sam said stoutly. " You and Dan go on by the path."

This time Susan did not hesitate at all. " Not by yourself you won't, Sam ! Anything might happen to you. We're coming too, Dan, and then, if anything did happen to one of us, there'd still be someone to run on and stop that train. We *must* stop the train."

" We must ! Mother's on it," Dan declared with a set little face.

" Come on, then. Into the tunnel ! " Sam said, seizing Susan by the hand and hurrying her along the line, for there was no time to lose.

Into the murky smoky darkness of the tunnel they dashed, afraid, but grimly holding on. The light from Sam's torch flickered palely and unevenly over the sleepered track. The battery was not very strong and the light did little more than illuminate a small circle around their feet as they ran.

" Oh, if only we could see better where we were going ! " Susan cried, her voice echoing eerily in the tunnel and making it seem still more dreadful.

" Hold on to me, Susan," Sam cautioned

her. " Keep within the light from the torch. Don't go too fast, Dan. Don't get ahead of the light like that."

Dan was forging ahead of Sam and Susan in his eagerness. " We must make it. We must ! " he cried.

Then, all of a sudden his foot caught in something and he fell heavily.

" Oh, Dan, are you hurt ? " Susan cried in a frenzy, trying to help him to rise.

" I tripped over a sleeper, that's all. I'm on my feet now," Dan said bravely, but as soon as he began to try to run again, his right foot gave way under him.

" Oh dear ! Oh dear ! I've twisted my foot. I can't walk," he cried.

" Oh, what shall we do now ! " Susan began almost to weep.

" I think I've sprained my ankle," Dan said in obvious pain.

" If the train comes now it might run into us all," Susan cried in panic.

" We've *got* to stop that train," Sam said with grim determination. " Dr. Brydon's on it." He shone his torch upon the blackened wall of the tunnel. Was it an illusion, or did one part of it seem even blacker than the other ? " Wait a second ! I'm right ! " he exclaimed in triumph. " There's a place hollowed out in the wall here for the men working on the railway to stand in when the train passes. You and Dan must wait here, Susan, and I'll run on alone. It can't be far to the end of the tunnel now."

They helped Dan into the recess in the wall, but as soon as he was comfortably propped into a sitting position with his back against the wall, he said : "Susan, you *must* go on with Sam. I'll stay here by myself. I shall be quite all right. But if Sam was alone and he tripped up, there would be no one to stop the train. Both of you must go ! Go on, now ! There's no time to stop and argue." He gave them both a gentle push.

"Come on, Susan. Dan's right ! Run ! " Sam said, pulling her along by his free hand and shining the torch with the other.

They had barely gone another hundred yards or so when Susan suddenly gasped, " Oh dear ! "

"What's the matter ? " Sam said in dread.

"I've got a stitch in my side. I can't go so fast. You must go on by yourself, Sam," Susan managed to tell him in jerks.

"I'm not leaving you," Sam said determinedly, slowing his pace a little. "Come on, Susan. Try to keep going."

Setting her teeth, and with her breath coming in tearing sobs, Susan bravely plodded on. They had barely covered twenty yards, however, when Sam gave a cry of joy. "Oh look! There's the end of the tunnel! It's not far now."

Ahead of them a pale oval of daylight began to grow in size as they ran towards it, and all around them the blackness began to give way to a grey dim light.

"Oh, thank goodness!" Susan gasped, as Sam dragged her along with him.

In another couple of minutes they emerged into the daylight, and Sam let go of Susan's hand.

"Here's the end of the tunnel at last, and look, there's the signal-box, barely two hundred yards ahead. I'll leave you now, Susan, and sprint for it." Sam gathered all his remaining strength for the last effort.

"Take my beret. It's red," Susan cried, snatching it from her head and thrusting it into Sam's hand. "Wave it as you run. They may see it from the signal-box."

Striding ahead, Sam made his final dash to reach the signal-box in time to stop the train.

Tom Whittaker in the signal-box happened to throw a glance over his shoulder in the direction of the tunnel.

"Eh, Bill, look up the line yonder," he said to his mate in the signal-box, Bill Arkwright. "Two kids have just come running out of the tunnel."

" Well, the little monkeys ! " Bill exclaimed in disapproval. " They ought to be spanked. You just can't keep bairns from trespassing. Supposing t'train from Preston had come along just now ! It's just about due, if it hadn't been three minutes late at Walton."

Tom Whittaker was staring at the children. " It's a little lad and a wench. Watch ! He's running on ahead of her and he's waving something red in his hand. Eh, Bill, he's heading straight this way. I think he's trying to signal us."

Bill joined Tom at the window. " Aye, you're right. He's waving at us wi' that red thing. 'Appen he's just making game of us."

" Nay, he's not ! " Tom exclaimed. " He's coming right here." He flung open a window and called down to Sam, " Eh, lad, what's up ? "

" Stop the train—the train coming out of Preston ! " Sam panted. " The river's burst its banks and it's altered its course and it's sweeping the embankment away below the tunnel. Do stop the train ! Oh, stop the train ! "

Tom Whittaker turned in excitement to Bill. " Eh, Bill, did you hear that ? T' river's washing the embankment away in Sykes' Hollow. Put the signals over to

' Danger,' quick ! Stop the train ! It's too late to 'phone Walton now. The train's left."

Bill sprang to the levers and jerked them over. " All right, Tom. The signals are at danger now. I only hope Dick Johnson is keeping a good look-out on the engine."

Sam, by this time, was making his way up the steps to the signal-box, and Bill hastened to help him in, for it was quite plain that Sam had reached the limit of his endurance.

" Here comes the little lass running too," Tom said.

" Oh, have you stopped the train ? " Susan panted. " Are we in time ? "

" I hope so, my little wench. The signals are set at danger. It's up to the engine-driver now. He always slows down as he approaches the tunnel anyway, so he's not very likely to overrun the signals," he added, seeing Susan's anxious look.

" You're two plucky little bairns to come through the tunnel like that," Bill told them.

" There wasn't time to come by the road or we'd have been too late," Sam explained. " Dan's in the tunnel yet."

" Dan ? " Bill said, lifting his eyebrows.

" He's my brother," Susan explained in her turn. " He fell and twisted his ankle, so we left him in a hollow in the wall and ran on."

" We'll have him out in no time," Tom

promised her, taking a stride towards the door, but he was stopped by Bill.

" Steady on ! Here comes the train. Eh, has Dick seen the signal ? Is she going to stop ? " He hung out of the window of the signal-box in a fever of apprehension. To everyone's thankful relief the train began to slow down and to come to a standstill.

" She's stopping right opposite the signal-box, praise be ! " said Bill.

As the train came to a halt the engine-driver shouted up to Tom Arkwright : " Eh, Tom, what's up ? What are the signals at danger for ? "

" You can't go on, lad. T' river's washing away the embankment and the line down in Sykes' Hollow," Tom called down to him.

Instantly windows and doors all up and down the train were opened and heads poked out. Sam and Susan went down on to the line and looked anxiously along the carriages for Dr. Brydon.

" What's the matter ? Why has the train stopped ? " people began to ask.

" The line's being washed away by floods from the river lower down," Tom began to explain to all and sundry. " This train's been saved by a miracle, I tell you. This little lad and wench ran through the tunnel to warn us just in time."

A head was thrust through the carriage window just opposite the two children.

"Susan! Sam Mitton! What are you doing here?" Susan's mother cried, as she opened the compartment door.

"Oh, Mother! Mother! Thank goodness it's you!" Susan sobbed with relief. "We've left Dan in the tunnel. He fell and sprained his ankle. We had to leave him there and run on and stop the train. Oh, Mother, do come to Dan."

In the twinkling of an eye Dr. Brydon was out of the train and had jumped on to the permanent way.

"If it isn't Dr. Brydon from Milchester!" Tom cried, recognizing her. "That's providential, ma'am. Come on, Bill. Get your big torches, and you and Dick must go into the tunnel with Dr. Brydon to get the little lad. I'll stay here and send out signals to Walton and along the line in the other direction to let them know what's happened."

Bill seized a couple of powerful torches, and he and Dick, together with Dr. Brydon and two passengers, set off back into the tunnel with Sam and Susan to find Dan.

"Da-an! Da-an!" they cried as they went, and their voices went echoing all through the tunnel, and it was only a matter of seconds before they heard Dan shouting back : " Hallo ! Hallo ! I'm here. Did you stop the train ? "

" Yes, Dan, it's all right," Susan cried as they came up to him. " The train's come to a stop just outside the tunnel, and here's Mother."

" Oh, Mother ! Mother ! " Dan almost sobbed as her arms went round him.

" Steady, Dan dear. It's all right now. No one's hurt and the train's saved. Let me have a look at that ankle."

Bill directed the light from his torch upon it at close range, while Dr. Brydon felt it gently all over.

" Ooh ! " Dan said, wincing a little.

" Yes, it hurts a bit when I touch it, I know, but I don't think there are any bones broken," his mother said reassuringly. " It's just a very uncomfortable sprain. But we shall have to get you out of here and the foot treated as soon as possible, before it swells too much."

" That's all right, ma'am. Me and Dick'll take him in our arms like in a chair. Now, Dan lad, put an arm round each of our necks and we'll lift you. Steady does it. That's grand. Now, Dr. Brydon, ma'am, will you and the bairns lead the way out with the torches."

Slowly the little procession made its way to the mouth of the tunnel, where a crowd of anxious passengers had gathered. A spontaneous cheer went up when they emerged, a cheer that came from many thankful hearts at the thought of the peril they had been spared.

" Sam, will you run ahead now and 'phone from the signal-box to Milchester Station ? Get the stationmaster to ring up Beechacres, and ask Mrs. Hallam to relay the message to Miss Marsden. Tell her what has happened, and ask her to bring the shooting-brake to the point on the road nearest to this signal-box," Dr. Brydon directed Sam. " In that way we'll all get home quickly."

" Right, Dr. Brydon, I will," Sam said, setting off at once.

" Explain exactly how Miss Marsden is to get to us," Dr. Brydon called after him.

" Aye. I'll think on it," the faithful Sam promised.

At One Elm Cottage Miss Marsden had just returned from decorating the stall in the marquee, where Roger and Ruth and Simon were still busy helping to arrange other exhibition stands and put up flags and bunting. Miss Marsden was a little disappointed when she found the cottage empty and not even the kettle singing on the hob. She had thought cheerfully about that welcome cup of tea all the way home in the rain, and it was rather a shock to find that faithful Susan was missing, and no tea was prepared for her.

" No one back yet ! Where can everyone be ? And in all this rain too," Marsdie said to herself. " Perhaps everyone is over at Beechacres." With her usual ready philosophy Marsdie began to set the table. Suddenly she paused in her operations and remarked, " Perhaps I'd better get ahead with the pickles. There isn't very much time. There'll be the beetroot to boil first. I can put that on to be cooking while I go on getting the tea ready."

She reached down a pan from the shelf and slipped the beetroot into it, and placed it over the lighted gas ring, but before she could do anything else, the bell of the connecting telephone between Beechacres and One Elm Cottage began to ring, and Marsdie hastened to answer it. " Oh dear ! " she said, as she ran into the kitchen. " That bell would go just when I was beginning to get busy." Then she heard Mrs. Hallam's voice at the other end, and for a moment Miss Marsden had difficulty in making out from Mrs. Hallam's excited voice just what had happened.

" Yes ? Sam Mitton ? Dan and Susan ? Dr. Brydon ! From a signal-box on the railway ? I don't understand ! " she exclaimed in a bewildered voice, then, as she began to grasp what Mrs. Hallam was trying to tell her. " Yes—yes ! Ran through the tunnel ? Saved the train ? Thank goodness Dr. Brydon is all right ! What's that ? Dan hurt ? Oh dear ! Only slightly. What a relief ! Yes, please ask the stationmaster to 'phone back at once to say I'll be along with the car as soon as I can get it out of the garage. Good-bye."

The 'phone bell tinkled as Marsdie hung up the receiver and tore off her overall.

" Oh dear ! I must go at once. The beet-root will be all right if I leave it on a low light like that till I come back." She cast a back-ward glance over her shoulder at the stove as she hurried out to find her raincoat. " I do wish Ruth and Roger had been home," she said to herself. " I'd better leave the back door key with Mrs. Hallam in case they come back before I return. Where's the garage key ? Ah, here in my pocket all the time." Marsdie breathed a sigh of relief that it was not missing just at the crucial moment as usually hap-pened, and saying, " That's everything," she closed the door behind herself, locked it, and sped away through the green door to deposit the key with Mrs. Hallam and to take the car out.

Some twenty minutes later Ruth and Roger rounded the corner of the house and found to their astonishment that the door was locked.

" Oh dear, Roger ! Everyone must be out. The back door's fastened, and now we can't get in, and just look how the rain is drenching down," Ruth exclaimed in exasperation.

" That's queer." Roger was perplexed. " Marsdie finished decorating the stall in the big marquee ages ago, and she said she was coming home for her tea and to make the pickles."

" Perhaps she's slipped across to Mrs. Hallam's for some ingredient she's forgotten. Look under the big paving stone and see if she has left the key," Ruth suggested.

Roger looked under the stone but there was no key there.

Suddenly Ruth stopped and began to sniff the air.

" Roger, can you smell something very queer—like—like *burning* ? " she asked.

Roger sniffed too. " Gosh ! Yes ! " He darted round the corner of the house. " I say, Ruth, there are fumes and smoke simply pouring through the ventilating window in the scullery," he cried.

Ruth hastened to him. " Oh dear ! Whatever's happened ? Is the house on fire ? " she cried.

" Let's hope Dan and Sam haven't blown something up again," Roger said.

Ruth suddenly clasped her hands in apprehension. " Oh, Roger, do you think Marsdie's had an accident and is lying gassed or suffocated in the scullery ? "

" My goodness ! What an awful thought ! " Roger cried, thoroughly alarmed. " We must get in at once, Ruth."

" But how ? " Ruth cried. " That little scullery window isn't big enough, and there isn't a window open anywhere else but in the bedrooms."

" Then a bedroom window it will have to be," Roger decided.

" But you can't go through that ! " Ruth exclaimed in alarm.

" Yes, I can ! " Roger said doggedly. " I must ! I'm going to swarm up this drain pipe in the corner."

He pointed to a drain pipe in the angle of the wall, the joints of which provided a good foothold. In a moment he was swarming up it towards the open window. " We can't risk anything happening to Marsdie," he said.

Ruth watched him in an agony of apprehension. " Oh, do be careful, Roger," she begged him.

" It's all right, Ruth. It's not terribly difficult," Roger reassured her.

" I shall have a fit if you fall," Ruth said.

" Nothing to the one I shall have ! " Roger said grimly. " All right, Ruth. I've reached the window-sill. Thank goodness the window's opened at the bottom and I can put a leg right over the sill." In a moment Roger had the window raised and was safely inside the room, to Ruth's great relief. " I'll be downstairs in a jiffy," he promised.

" Oh, Roger, be quick, be quick ! We must save Marsdie," Ruth urged.

In another minute Roger appeared at the kitchen window, laughing uproariously.

" Marsdie's not here," he cried as he flung open the sash. " It's all right, Ruth. No one's here, and I've turned the gas off. There's no key in the door at all, so you'll have to make an unceremonious entrance through the kitchen window. Give me your hand and step up on to the sill."

In a trice he had Ruth whisked through the window and standing beside him. Through the open scullery door the fumes poured, and the smoke eddied about them.

" Oh, Roger, what is it ? I can hardly see you for smoke. Oh, what a smell, too ! And where's Marsdie ? "

Roger laughed. " Goodness knows ! She's certainly not lying flat out in the scullery. But there is evidence that our Marsdie has certainly been here." Almost helpless with laughter, Roger led the way to the scullery.

" What is it, Roger ? There's a queer

earthy smell mingled with all the smoke," Ruth exclaimed.

"Come over to the gas stove, Ruth, if you can fight your way through all the fumes," Roger said.

Coughing and sneezing they made their way to the stove.

"Now look at that, but don't touch it," Roger said, indicating a pan from which the fumes emanated.

"Why, the pan's practically red-hot, and there are some black charred lumps at the bottom. What are they?"

"*Marsdie's beetroot!*" Roger said. "There's no water in that pan!"

They both broke down and held their sides in hysterical laughter.

"Thank goodness it's nothing worse," Ruth said as they began to recover. "But poor Marsdie! Her pickles!"

"She'll hardly take a first prize with these," Roger commented. "We'd better open the windows and the door and let these fumes out."

Just at that moment the door opened and Mrs. Hallam dashed into the kitchen.

"Eh, Ruth, whatever's happening? I thought the house was on fire when I saw the smoke pouring out. I came to bring the key Miss Marsden left with me."

"It's all right, Mrs. Hallam," Roger reassured her. "It's just Marsdie again. It's her new way of making pickles!"

"She put them in the pan *without any water*," Ruth explained.

"Eh, poor Miss Marsden!" Mrs. Hallam commiserated. "That's what happened with having to rush off in such a hurry to fetch Dan."

"Oh, what's happened to Dan?" Ruth asked in a startled voice.

"He fell and sprained his ankle when they were running to stop the train."

"Stop the train? Whatever for? Where were they?" Roger asked.

In a few minutes Mrs. Hallam had told them the whole of the story.

"Oh, Roger, that was Mother's train!" Ruth cried, clutching him by the arm.

"Thank goodness they had the pluck to run through the tunnel!" Roger said.

Just then there was the sound of a motor horn and the car drawing up outside.

"Here they come!" Mrs. Hallam said.

"I'll go and help to carry Dan in," Roger said, rushing out to the car.

"I'll pull out the settee for him," Ruth said.

"And I'll put the kettle on if I can see mi way to the gas stove," Mrs. Hallam announced. "We shall all want a cup of tea after this 'ere."

It was a very jolly tea party which was held at One Elm Cottage that day. Sam and Susan were called upon more than once to tell their story all over again, while Dan, his foot now securely bandaged and comfortable, reclined on the settee and was ministered to by everyone present, while he beamed beatifically upon them.

" Another cup of tea, Dr. Brydon ? " Mrs. Hallam said, officiating by common consent at the teapot.

" Thanks, Mrs. Hallam. I never knew a cup of tea to be so welcome," Dr. Brydon declared.

" I don't need to ask Miss Marsden. I know what the answer will be," Mrs. Hallam said, stretching out her hand for Marsdie's cup.

" Here's Simon back already ! " Ruth said as she heard a step outside. Simon came in, a little warm and breathless after hurrying.

" It's all right, Dan. I've been to the marquee and seen Mr. Benton, and he says your rabbit-hutch can go to the marquee at *any* time. They're quite willing to relax the rule in your and Sam's case," he announced. " Milchester people seem to want to acclaim you as heroes."

" There was nowt to it, Simon," Sam said modestly. " But I'm glad about not being too late with the rabbit-hutch. Will you give me a hand to carry it down after tea, Simon ? "

" Willingly, Sam."

" I'm jolly glad we can still show our rabbit," Dan said, very pleased. " I *was* worrying about that all the time I was sitting in the tunnel."

" Why, bless the lad ! " Mrs. Hallam cried. " Sitting in the middle of a tunnel in the dark and all he worried about was a rabbit ! Well, as my mother used to say——"

" And she was a wise woman ! " the Brydons chorused as one man with their usual vigour.

" ' Heaven sends t'little things to worry us so as we can forget about t'big uns '," Mrs. Hallam went on, blissfully disregarding the interruptions.

" That's very true, Mrs. Hallam," Marsdie replied. " Well, it's a good thing everything has ended so well and happily."

" Except your pickles, Marsdie ! " Ruth reminded her slyly.

" Yes, except my pickles ! " Marsdie agreed mournfully. " Now nobody will ever believe I'm a wizard at making pickles."

" Marsdie's new recipe for pickled beetroot ! Take some beetroots. Drop them in a pan. Roast them till they're red hot . . ." Roger began to declaim in fun.

" Now, stop your teasing, Roger Brydon," Mrs. Hallam interrupted him. " Here ! Let me have a look at those beetroots."

Ruth brought the pan for her inspection. The beetroots were by now almost cold.

" Eh, do you know what I think, Miss Marsden ? " Mrs. Hallam asked. " They're only burnt on the *outside*."

" But that spoils them quite enough for pickles, Mrs. Hallam," Miss Marsden lamented.

" Nay, I'm not so sure." Mrs. Hallam shook her head. " Give me a knife and let me cut through this little one." She suited the action to the word and displayed the result proudly. " There ! Look ! Why, it's lovely inside. You know what happens when you roast a joint of meat ? You put it in a very hot oven first of all for a few minutes to seal it off."

" Oh, yes, and that keeps all the juices and goodness inside," Ruth corroborated.

" Aye, that's it, Ruth. And that's just what has happened here. The beetroots are all sealed off on the outside. Just drop them in a pan again, Miss Marsden . . . only this time put some water in . . . and boil 'em a bit longer."

" And then they'll be as tender as Mrs. Hallam's heart," Roger teased.

" Eh, Roger, if I get hold of you, you'll find I'm as hard as those beetroots are on the outside, even if my heart is tender," Mrs. Hallam threatened him.

"You've given me new heart about my pickles, Mrs. Hallam," Miss Marsden said. "Yes, I will boil the beetroot up again and see what it's like when it's sliced. It can't be any worse than it seems to be anyway, and I might be able to use it, even if it isn't good enough for the competition."

"You wait and see first, before you give up hope," Mrs. Hallam advised her. "As my mother used to say, ' Use what you have and you'll never want ', and she was a real wise woman, she was," Mrs. Hallam said, getting her proverbial saying in without interruption this time. "Well, I've still got the finishing touches to put to my cake, so I'll see you all to-morrow at the Milchester Show," she added, patting Dan on the head on her way out.

The Milchester Show the next day presented a very gay scene, for after that last heavy thunderstorm the rain had cleared, and the Saturday proved to be a warm and sunny day, with a gentle wind that dried the wet grass and helped to repair the damage done by the previous day's rain. The Milchester Prize Band, with Grandfather Mitton valiantly playing on the trombone, gave gay selections and popular marches, and everyone felt very cheerful and light-hearted. At last the band performance came to an end, and everyone gathered in the big marquee to hear the Chairman's speech and to see the competition awards being made.

After a few opening remarks, the Chairman came straight away to what most people were really impatient to hear.

" And now it is my very great pleasure to announce the results of the awards in the prize competitions. I will deal with the Handicraft Competition first, as this had the largest number of entries. There was a record number, and the judges had the greatest difficulty in coming to any decision, so they decided to lump all the prize money together and award it to St. Jonathan's Convalescent Hospital for the very best collection of handicrafts they have ever seen."

Tumultous applause greeted this very popular decision.

" Oh, Marsdie, isn't that grand ? " Simon exulted.

" Lovely, Simon. Now everyone at St. Jonathan's will be happy and there will be no heart-burnings," Marsdie said, very pleased.

" It's a feather in *your* cap. You taught them, Marsdie," Susan whispered.

The Chairman went on : " In the live-stock section devoted to rabbits, the prize has been won by Dan Brydon and Sam Mitton for their exhibit, Peter the Giant."

There was a burst of clapping from everyone in the marquee.

" And I might say," the Chairman went on, " that if it had not been for Sam Mitton, and Dan and Susan Brydon some of us who travel by train might not have been able to come here so happily to-day."

The cheers that followed would have raised the roof, if the marquee had had one. Dan and Sam and Susan hung their heads modestly and tried to hide behind their friends.

" And that brings me to the knitting competition. In this, Mrs. Fawcett was adjudged first, with Miss Susan Brydon a close second."

There was more clapping, and Ruth hugged Susan joyfully. Her turn was to come next, however.

" Now for the competition for the best iced cake," the Chairman went on. " The judges could not come to a decision about this either, so they decided to divide the first three prizes equally among Mrs. Benton, Mrs. Hallam, and Miss Ruth Brydon, without any distinction of place."

" Eh, well done, Ruth love, I am glad," Mrs. Hallam exclaimed.

" So am I, Mrs. Hallam. I'm glad we're both together after all," Ruth said, as she linked her arm in that of Mrs. Hallam.

But the biggest surprise of all was yet to come.

" In the class for preserves and pickles, the first prize is awarded to Miss Marsden for a jar of pickled beetroot. The judge said she had never seen better-coloured nor more tender beetroot, and there must have been great care and skill in the boiling of them."

There were shouts of laughter from the Brydon family, almost drowned by the storm of applause for Miss Marsden, who blushed furiously, for she had never guessed how popular she was in Milchester.

" First *roast* your beetroot, Marsdie—or was it the Tickling Spice that did the trick ? " Roger whispered in her ear. " Anyway, I crown you Queen of Pickles, Marsdie. But you'd better warn the Fire Brigade next time you start pickling."

" You shall stand by instead with the garden hose, Roger," Marsdie chuckled. " Be quiet now. The Chairman's going on."

In the succeeding awards, Roger and Simon found they had not fared too badly, and had carried off a second prize for runner beans and a third for cabbages.

After the Show was over, however, there ensued a riotous time of selling the exhibits for the Brydons, for, without exception, any-one whose entry was of a perishable or eatable description had passed it on to Miss Marsden's stall as a gift to be sold. In addition, many hand-made articles from the Crafts exhibits found their way on to the stall, given by generous friends of St. Jonathan's.

It was a very happy little band of workers who counted up the takings at the close of that day.

" All those lovely things to be given to St. Jonathan's ! It really is incredible ! " Marsdie said with a beaming face.

" It was wonderful," Dr. Brydon agreed. " I never knew Milchester people to fail us, though, in their generosity."

" How much money have we made, **Mr.** Cameron ? " Roger asked.

" Well over a hundred pounds already, and I haven't done counting yet," was the answer.

" Then will you kindly add this to it, please, Mr. Cameron," came a voice over his shoulder. It belonged to Mr. Erskine, the Chairman of the Milchester Show.

" A cheque ! " Mr. Cameron exclaimed in surprise.

"Yes. Perhaps you would read aloud the note which accompanies it ? " Mr. Erskine asked.

" With compliments from grateful passengers on the 5.3 train," Mr. Cameron read to the assembled group.

" Oh, what a splendid thought ! " Marsdie cried, hugging Susan.

" It's marvellous ! And to think I was a

passenger on that train and nobody told me a thing about it ! What a well-kept secret ! " Dr. Brydon said.

" Whatever shall we do with all this money, Dr. Brydon ? " Mr. Cameron asked.

" It would buy some splendid sun-ray lamps, which would be a great help in treating the children during the winter," Dr. Brydon suggested.

" That's an excellent idea," Marsdie approved. " Out of the rain came sunshine for our little patients after all."

Dan and Sam winked at each other, and Susan intercepted the wink.

" In a way it really came out of Dan and Sam's explosion," she said.

" How was that ? " Mr. Cameron asked with interest.

Dan looked rather self-conscious. " I was vexed with Roger for calling us ' priceless idiots ' when the flask exploded, so Sam and I decided we'd go fishing instead of helping arrange things at the Show," he said rather reluctantly.

" And that's how we came to see what happened at the river," Sam added to the explanation. " Only it was jolly lucky Susan came along when she did."

" It seems to me that everyone had a hand in this particular pie," Mr. Cameron chuckled.

" Say rather in this particular pot of pickles, Mr. Cameron," Roger corrected him with a grin, bowing in theatrical fashion at Marsdie.

" Well, as my mother used to say, and she was a wise woman," Mrs. Hallam said quickly, getting it all in before anyone could stop her, " it isn't the ingredients by themselves that make a good dish. It's the way they're all put together ! It's the same with the Brydons' pickles, I'm thinking."